ABDUCTED BY
CIRCUMSTANCE

Fiction by David Madden

Novels
The Beautiful Greed
Cassandra Singing
Brothers in Confidence
Bijou
The Suicide's Wife
Pleasure-Dome
On the Big Wind
Sharpshooter

Short Story Collections
The Shadow Knows
The New Orleans of Possibilities

ABDUCTED BY CIRCUMSTANCE

A NOVEL

David Madden

THE UNIVERSITY OF TENNESSEE PRESS / KNOXVILLE

"A Cry of Ice," by David Madden, copyright 2006 by David Madden. First published in *New Letters* 72, nos. 3–4 (2006). It is printed here with the permission of *New Letters* and the Curators of the University of Missouri–Kansas City.

The paper in this book meets the requirements of American National Standards Institute / National Information Standards Organization specification Z39.48-1992 (Permanence of Paper). It contains 30 percent post-consumer waste and is certified by the Forest Stewardship Council.

Library of Congress Cataloging-in-Publication Data

Madden, David, 1933–
Abducted by circumstance: a novel / David Madden. — 1st ed.
        p. cm.
ISBN-13: 978-1-57233-701-5
ISBN-10: 1-57233-701-X
1. Abduction—Fiction.
2. Alexandria Bay (N.Y.)—Fiction.
I. Title.

PS3563.A339A65 2010
813'.54—dc22
2009039641

ABDUCTED BY
CIRCUMSTANCE

1

She heard seagulls.

She looked up. Where are they?

Children onshore whining, carried over the ice?

No. Women, wailing.

No. Seagulls, crying.

She looked down at Melissa. "Do you see—?"

Melissa shook her head, put a finger to her lips, pointed another finger down.

The ice on the lake was heaving, like a sleeping person's chest—ice breaking up down there, crying out in the twilight, like seagulls, children, women, snow beginning to come down, lightly.

The stout man wearing the snow mask still stood on the porch of the defunct fog house, under the black horns, hunched over, looking out over the lake, his head still moving, as if searching for someone out there on the ice that heaved and sank, cracked, cried.

A tall woman suddenly appeared—wearing an open, elegant brown coat, hatless, stepping up onto the observation deck, as if onto a stage, with the air of a person aware that people are often glad to see her coming, impressed by the very sight of her. She seemed to think she was alone, stood erect against the subzero wind chill, gazing out over Lake Ontario, awed, smiling sublimely.

Do you hear the cries yet? Carol surprised herself that she had spoken to the lady, as clearly as if aloud.

The lady looked up at the sky, filling up with swirling snow.

To get her face out of the scalding wind, Carol reached out for Melissa's hand and helped her walk over yesterday's compacted snow back to the lighthouse wall.

Her watch declared that she would get home late again, her husband, Jack, would already be on his way home—from wherever he had gone—one of his Saturday activities.

Up against the white wall, a long sealed crack, Carol looked around the curve of the tower to gaze at the woman's profile, skin tanned or naturally dark, hair jet black.

Carol smiled. The hope of experiencing rare moments such as this was what had made her scoop Melissa up and go out to the car and hit the highway.

She watched the lady's flowing gestures. Not a performance. Not even a focused event for this tall lady, but out of a natural flow of her confidence and energy and everyday good humor.

Carol was glad she had come, as if she had set out to watch this lady in this place. Her sudden excursions when her husband was out were not to watch, but simply to go, to be gone, going anywhere, as far away as any given free time would allow. As palpable as the cold wind, she felt how different this excursion was, watching a strange woman being herself, a woman on her way somewhere, probably not back home, even though it was late for starting a trip, a woman who was not getting away from the house, who always did exactly what she wanted to do, even when it was necessary.

Toss your hair back again.

Like that.

The lady took a short step forward, flinging her coat back to free her hip where she rested the back of her hand, one arm akimbo, then a bigger step backward. In the other hand her keys hung—a little shake just now, as if eager for the ignition again, to get going again, but not impatient, content for the moment to anticipate.

Carol saw that her first impression, that the lady was about her own age, was wrong, maybe the black hair was dyed, but not a wig—no, not wig-looking, even if it were a wig. Once natural black, complementing the skin that had

2

always been olive. Greek? No. Possibly Italian. Probably not. Maybe Turkish, Istanbul. Most likely Argentinean. Long legs. High heels.

The look of her was of a woman who could carry off any whim, but not a woman of mere whim, a purposeful woman, most of the time, a career woman, not a housewife, except when she wanted to play that role, too. Maybe even a churchwoman, too, but one who surprises fellow parishioners that she would take time off to participate in routine church affairs.

She is turning, no, she is pivoting, like Jack showing Tim how soldiers do an about-face—no, Jack, *you* get out of this picture!—and she walked or strode, as if going down a hallway to an important meeting with her subordinates, who were always pumped up for her entrance, to the opposite side of the observation deck with a direct look toward Canada.

An instant intuition made Carol feel as if she knew this lady, had known her a good long while, had at least seen her sometime, somewhere, before.

Turning away from the wind that stung her face, pulling Melissa closer, watching the snowflakes become larger, she gazed in her mind upon the afterimage of the stylish lady's walk, so confident, enhanced by the high heels.

Carol imagined how this lovely lady would look turning away from Canada, walking toward *her,* and, as she got closer, redolent of Shalimar.

One more actual look before she lifted Melissa up into her arms and must go back to the house, hoping to beat Jack.

The lady was swinging her body, her coattails swirling, coming down the icy steps on high heels. Here she comes, here she comes right toward me, not seeming to see me.

Carol stepped back, as if to make room for the lady against the white wall.

"Mother! I cut myself! It's blood!"

Carol turned left, setting to the side of her own life the tall lady's vibrant image, and leaned down to look at Melissa, who'd thrust out her thumb.

She sucked off the blood, seeing even in the dim light it was a minor cut, made by the already broken kaleidoscope Melissa's chilled red hands had dropped in the snow. "All better?"

"All better." Melissa whimpered theatrically.

Carol turned back around, to catch another, last glimpse of the lady.

The observation platform steps were vacant.

Where did she go?

Where is she?

Where are you, Lady?

Desiring one more look, Carol lifted Melissa and turned toward the vacant lighthouse keeper's cottage and the driveway—the lady was not walking over there.

The pickup parked there when she drove up was roaring down the curve onto the narrow road, making new tracks in the snow, tires squealing in the icy slush, shooting onto the road into the blowing snow that now darkened the lake.

The man who wore the snow mask was not standing under the black foghorn on the porch of the defunct fog house.

Behind Carol's old Oldsmobile, snow almost had disfigured what looked a little like a Mercedes.

She yanked the back door of the Oldsmobile to shatter its seal of ice and lifted Melissa inside, closed the door, and hurried back up to the lighthouse, walking in the woman's original footsteps.

Hoping the woman would be leaning there, that she would turn and smile, Carol walked around the tower. Having walked around the tower again, she walked around the foghorn house, past its porch.

Lady, you did not know that a man wearing a snow mask stood on the porch behind you.

"My pistol is aimed at your back, Lady. Don't say a word. Turn around and look at the pistol. Walk quickly to that pickup in the driveway and get in. I am right behind you."

Suddenly aware that she had been talking aloud, as if directly to the lady, Carol spoke to her more deliberately, more clearly in her imagination. You did not panic. You did as he told you, at first, walked to the pickup truck. The shock of his body, full length and force of it—a sudden blow up against your back. His knees connect with the backs of your knees, make you buckle, in the same instant his left arm smacks your windpipe, you gasp, a tight, sharp gasp, his other hand over your mouth, smelling of old grease, because no matter how often he washes them, he can never get that smell out of the seams of his palms or his pants, his shirts, he whirls you around to shove you into his pickup, the door cracked open, ready, and you react so quickly, it is *he* who is most startled, by *you,* who looked to him older than the other women, more vulnerable, easier to handle, even though he did notice the power in your athletic grace, thought he was ready for what it might do to his method, and your elbow stabs his ribs, but he's all muscle, and takes surprise blows like maybe in a karate class, and he does not imagine you will do what you do next, dip deeper in the knees, thrust your right leg backward between his legs, stick your right foot behind his left foot—he's wearing boots—and twist, pivoting inward on your left toe, just like those Chinese women in the cheap martial arts videos my husband is addicted to, that's when he knows he has to slug your handsome face or abort, but it's you who takes karate, can take a punch, even so, it knocks you off balance, your back slams up against the truck bed, you kick at his groin but misfire, he shoulders you on *in,* through the door, and you splay out on the floorboard, the passenger seat ripped out, kicking, trying to strike his shin, trying to find his groin, but he slugs and slaps you again and again, stuns you, turns you over and, just as you think you can press your knees against the floor and thrust yourself upward, he gets a grip on your left arm just above the wrist, you feel something tighter than a hand, ice cold, hear a rattle of steel, know it's handcuffs, bitch! bitch! cunt! erupts from deep in his chest, you can't jerk loose of some kind of anchor—an eyebolt in the floor, the other handcuff locked on it, you feel parts of his chest, arms, legs slipping off your body, dimly see his body backing away, the door slams, shuts you in. You hope someone has been watching. I wish now I had been watching. My six-year-old distracted me.

Realizing she had been standing stock still too long, she hurried back down to the driveway to look inside the lady's car. I should have looked there first.

Standing by the car, she again imagined, felt the lady being seized, lifted, shut up in the truck.

She brushed the snow off the Mercedes window on the passenger's side.

The lady's briefcase lay on the seat, upright, slightly tilted.

She tried the door handle. Locked.

Running up the driveway to her own car, she wished she had brought the cell phone her father had given her for Christmas. "For emergency use, Carol."

She looked into the Oldsmobile backseat. Melissa was still there, a slouched, deeply asleep rag doll, the broken kaleidoscope in her lap.

Seeing the image of the pickup truck shooting out of the parking lot, she told Melissa to buckle herself into the child restraint, and jumped behind the wheel.

She set off in pursuit of the snow-masked man's black pickup truck, now white with snow, like all vehicles now, slowing down for BLIND CHILD AREA.

"Too fast again, Mother."

Thick snowfall got her attention again, and she realized she was driving recklessly.

In an intuitive rush, Carol felt, in her very bones, her very spirit, that if she imagines what is happening to the lady, imagines how she is reacting, and if she keeps on talking to her, she will somehow be helping her feel, do, and say what will help her gain time, escape, survive.

Like everybody else, especially women, Lovely Lady, you have been watching the news for the past six years, seen the late breaking news when they show the police cars parked on the bank of the river under the International Bridge, the big trucks whizzing by on the long two-lane span above, the ice mobiles whirling in and out and among the Thousand Islands, so you know where he is taking you, but you hope he doesn't take you there immediately, you hope you have some time, because they are still looking for the last woman abducted from Watertown last week.

Do not scream. That's what he wants. You know that their screaming thrills him. He shuts them up instantly by showing them the gun, maybe the buck knife, maybe only the biggest fist any woman ever drew back from. Found with their throats cut—all six of them, Watertown women. You have watched the news, leaning forward in your chair, as I have. Watched the bossy man on the TV who shows you what you must do to protect yourself, unless you're up against men who can do to you what he just did.

You are older than the others, but you have the same youthful vitality because of the kind of woman you are. You not screaming will get his attention, that you are not the same as the others. You know that he will expect you to behave the way he always daydreams it, that the others have not disappointed him, but he did not let them scream long because he took them from the middle of the city in broad daylight, had to act fast. Not screaming lets you think. You think—he has changed who, where, and when he strikes. He has taken you not from the city but from a remote place at land's end, on the edge of nowhere at twilight.

"Slow down." Melissa's deeper voice from the back seat. "Slowohdown."

He keeps looking over at you to see why you do not scream. Handcuffed to that eyebolt driven into the floorboard, you can only kneel, but you are tall, and he sees that you are not lying down into yourself, that you are up on your knees, your back straight, and when he quickly turns his head sidewise to check on you, your face is directly beside his, a foot away, as if you're saying, Look at me, look at my face.

He does look, into your eyes, then looks away.

You do not smile. Not yet. You know what your smile does to everybody. Even though it's natural for you, you know how it affects people. Dazzles. Save it, later.

On a stretch with no houses, Carol heard the ice breaking up, crying. No, didn't her window shut out the sound?

Passing through the village of Cape Vincent, she saw no trucks or cars ahead, none coming toward her.

In the village of Clayton, she pulled over to Lost Navigator Tavern.

"Why're we stopping here?"

"Just be still a second and let your mother think."

"I'm not hungry."

"Be still. Be still. . . . Be still."

Why *did* I stop here? Why here and not someplace else?

"You said let's go for a ride. It's not a ride. Nothing's to see *here*."

"Mommy needs to think."

"Well, are you thinking now?"

Yes, there's a pay phone inside.

As she waited for the Alexandria Bay police station to answer her ring, she realized that a patrol car would come to the house to question her and that the neighbors would ask her husband about it, that Jack would demand to know what she was doing with his six-year-old thirty or so miles west of Alexandria Bay on the edge of Lake Ontario in the blinding snow at the scene of a crime, and she knew she'd eventually get entangled and stuck in any web of lies she might weave.

Anonymous. Okay. Anonymous.

"Alexandria Bay Police Department. How can I help you this evening?" She recognized Frank's voice.

"A woman has been abducted at the Tibbetts Point Lighthouse." Would Frank recognize her voice?

"You need to call the Cape Vincent police, on that."

"Oh, I didn't know they had one. But, listen, act fast, call them yourself—and the highway patrol."

"Okay. Name, please."

"No, I am anonymous."

"Okay, on that. Then please describe the vehicle."

"A pickup."

"Color?"

"White—I mean, black, covered with snow."

"Any distinguishing marks?"

Like a birthmark? "No, all covered with snow."

"Describe the driver for me."

"I *can't* describe him for you!"

"Only natural you're afraid of him, on that, but we—"

"No, it's because I didn't actually see him. He wore a snow mask like a lot of people around here." She and Melissa would have worn masks, too, had the excursion not been impulsive.

"Where are you calling from, ma'am?"

"A public phone."

"Location?"

Carol hung up.

She drove up and down the few streets of the village, keen-eyed, on the lookout, passing a Clayton patrol car, lights flashing, talking silently to the lady in her imagination. You almost ask, Where are you taking me? But you don't, because that'd put the Thousand Islands in his head where he displays the corpses.

You say, Where are we going?

Sure enough, that makes him turn his head, and your eyes are right there looking into his. Where are *we* going, like you are saying to him, You and I are in this together—I am not the only one in a state of crisis.

None of your business, he says, and you almost laugh at the irony. He does that quick turn and looks and sees your smile this time, but it's not the smile that will disarm him, so to speak. Save that for exactly the right moment.

He says, You think this is funny?

The smile was a mistake, so you change the subject, with something he will not expect.

I wish I had one of Jreck's subs. I am so hungry, I could eat a horse. Are you hungry? Let me buy us a juicy sandwich, loaded.

"Who you talking to, Mother?"

"Was I talking?"

Bet you could be a black belt, but tonight you were clumsy, weren't you?

I'm not usually clumsy.

I could tell that by the graceful way you went for my nuts, you bitch.

He plays with words. That's your opening. You wanted to know, and now you know, that you can talk to him. Get him talking and keep him talking. But all the others were talkers, too. The head nurse. The yoga instructor. The advertising executive. I forget the others, I am ashamed to say. And now, you. Maybe he likes to talk. Or maybe he hates that. Be careful, Lady.

Will we have something to eat where we're going?

Shut up.

You shut up and look around.

Bitch, he says, like an afterthought.

Keep down on the floor.

The sound of the tires on the highway snow at sixty miles an hour makes you feel you are getting near the place he planned, you feel panic coming on, you stop talking.

What makes you think I might got food where we're going?

We, he said. Good.

We—you say—we could go some place where there's food and something to drink.

I *got* something to drink, he says, and takes a swig, goes *Ahhhhhh,* the way men love to do.

Gimme, why don't you?

You raise up as straight as you can and lean sideways toward him and lift your chin, hoping he doesn't kiss you.

He tips the bottle. You take a deep swig. Two people drinking together in a pickup on the highway in thick snowfall at first dark.

You think you can drink me under the table?

Maybe. You give him a husky half laugh.

We'll never know.

"At least you got him to saying *we.*"

"What?" As if Melissa heard more than Carole was saying.

"Nothing."

"It's the lighthouse again, Mother."

Absorbed in talking to the lady, Carol was surprised to realize that she was back at Tibbetts Point Lighthouse so quickly. To make certain.

The lady's car was still there, shapeless under the snow, all four doors forced, flung wide open.

The Clayton police car, light still flashing, was parked almost bumper to bumper. Two flashlights moving among the one, two, three lighthouse buildings.

Carol turned around and headed for her own house.

He takes you past WELCOME TO ALEXANDRIA BAY, THE HEART—a red heart— OF THE THOUSAND ISLANDS—which freeze and thaw each year.

He stops the pickup.

9

Oh, is this the old thorn grove? One of my very favorite places. All those boulders to climb over. I recognize that old blighted birch tree.

Hell, the place is infested with river rats big as foxes, woman.

Yes, but I used to sit on that very stump over there, and my favorite uncle sat beside me and told me whoppers about his fishing.

Yeah, sure, you know what they say about uncles and nieces.

Yes, but he was different. He never hurt anybody. You would have liked him.

How the hell would *you* know who would like me and who wouldn't? I'm talking too much.

One cannot talk too much.

One? One what?

You and me.

Hey, Lady, don't you smart women read the goddamn newspapers or watch TV?

He gets out and opens your door. Oh, a gentleman. A gentleman armed with a pistol and probably a knife, concealed.

You hope somebody will come by, somebody pull over and look down into the thorn thicket, some vigilant trucker with a cell phone.

But *I* am the only one who sees you. You don't *need* me, but I am here, making things go the way they are going. This is the way it *is* going, I know it, I know it. Well, going well. And you and I will make it end well.

His whole routine so far is not going as it always does. Six times before is not always, but six is only how many they have found, and DNA is a slow procedure.

You are one of a kind. He can tell. He's frustrated maybe, but he's just plain interested. Like me, like me.

But I must focus on *you,* not him.

You don't even have to think of what to say or do. You have a way of acting natural in all circumstances, anyway.

His fly is open.

You do not look away.

Your fly is unzipped.

He looks down.

Then you are looking into his eyes.

He looks up, shuts his eyes, zips his fly.

He sits on the floor, his back against the frame at the open door, his feet outside, and looks at your face quickly and looks away quickly, then back and forth slowly. He must think you are bold. It's not that he does not think you are afraid. He knows you have to be—under the circumstances. But he can't see it in your face, your eyes, your shoulders—not cringing—you aren't trembling or shrinking away from him.

He has broken his routine. They were all like you, vivacious, successful, but just vulnerable enough that they reacted as any abducted woman would react. But they were younger, under forty, you are older and different, you would never look vulnerable to anybody. Your failure to show fear disorients him. I'm not sure myself how you can look so cool and still be terrified, naturally, deep inside where he cannot see.

He reaches out to touch your hair. You do not cringe.

Dyed, ain't it?

Says *ain't* deliberately, to make you correct his grammar so he can get mad at you.

Only the few streaks of gray.

How the hell old *are* you?

I'll bet this is the first time you have ever asked a lady that question.

He stares at you—sees more clearly you *are* a lady, a little surprised.

Why don't I just leave you sitting on that rock over there, maybe handcuffed to that dead birch tree?

I've never had to fight off a coyote. But I guess there's always a first time.

He laughs.

You got him to laugh.

You laugh with him, louder, so the truck cab is full of it, and he can't help but feel it vibrate in his head. He stops, abruptly. So do you. But he's still looking at that smile.

On Highway 12, Seaway Trail, again, Carol passed shoals of sharp wire, the corrections facility.

As she hit that stretch named POW MIA HIGHWAY MEMORIAL, she saw the Alexandria patrol car coming at her. As it passed, she knew that Frank sat behind the slow windshield wipers of the Alexandria patrol car that was passing her, the New York State Highway Patrol car following him too close.

You watch him take out a cigarette, pop it in his mouth, the way he must have practiced as a kid starting to smoke. Before he can light it, you request one for yourself. He sticks that one in your mouth and takes out another one for himself and lights yours—the lady first—it falls out of your mouth, so he frees your right hand.

I'm left-handed.

He re-cuffs your right hand and un-cuffs your left hand.

Thank you.

You politely blow your smoke away from him.

He lights his own cigarette and blows the smoke away from you.

You can't help but cough, because, with that self-control of yours, you quit smoking years ago.

He looks at you suspiciously.

But you are a *you* to him now, not a bitch-cunt-*thing*. He relaxes with *you*, even in this near-zero cold. He looks as if he has not relaxed, really relaxed, like this in months. I guess that's my problem too. I haven't been able to relax in years. Distractions, distractions, always distractions! All the way to Alexandria Bay, I have had that image of the two of you relaxed in that vehicle, not relaxing doing this and that, just relaxed, not moving much, like a photograph so real it seems to move a little, vibrate.

I liked the hell out of the way you walked up on that observation deck, platform.

Thank you. I haven't really watched *you* walk.

I don't even know if I *have* a walk.

Well, shall we walk?

In the snow? In those high heels?

I love to walk in the snow, and not the first time in high heels.

This is not a good place.

You think, he's thinking that those searchers on ice mobiles might come ashore here.

We could go some place else, where there is a path.

Do you know a place like that?

Yes, many. But *you* choose.

Yeah, I know a place, too, just past Chippewa Bay, with a view of Dark Island and that Singer Castle in the river. I want to see you walk and smoke a cigarette with me and laugh. But you better not laugh too loud. I liked it when you laughed. I'm going to leave that hand free.

He cuffs your left hand to his right. So he's a left-handed smoker.

East of Chippewa, one mile below the lighthouse and the red lighthouse keeper's house, you will see a sign up ahead, BLIND BAY.

I will stay with you all the way, Lady, talk to you all the way.

"What lady?" Melissa was sounding aggravated now.

"Did I say something about a lady?"

As Carol turned up the steep hill and into the driveway, Melissa said from the backseat, "That ice on Lake Ontario sounded like a little girl crying in her sleep."

Like the lady. Like all his victims. Like my mother. The ice heaving like the chest of a human being, sleeping.

He isn't exactly taking *you* somewhere. You are going there together. To take a walk together at night, the wind still now, the sky clear, the moon full, so you will be able to see. You have done just what a woman who looked the way you did striding up to that platform, climbing those steps that way, smiling, and starting down again, *would do* under such circumstances. You fought him, but when he subdued you, you started slowly but surely to behave normally, as if you were not afraid of him. You did not look away, but looked him in the eye, to show you weren't looking at his face to testify against him, as if instead you were going along somewhere *with* him. Everything you did and said broke the pattern of the others, how they reacted. You have disoriented him, and he has had to relate to you until you became two people in a pickup smoking and then deciding together to go somewhere walking in a secluded place.

How many women could have done what you did, after watching the news and reading about the abductions, one by one, over the past six years?

Oh, listen! Hear the owls?

He looks startled. You think, Not because he has never heard an owl hooting at night but because no one ever asked him in that tone of voice to listen. He listens, his mouth open. You even dare to tell him to shut his eyes to hear better. He does.

It stopped. A tone of disappointment.

Maybe it will call out again.

You think, Beauty taming the beast. He is big, but, listening to a bird, he looks smaller. Even so, you know he may turn at any moment, anything can trigger them.

Like the outdoors woman you are—that natural tan—you are walking naturally in the woods, somewhere off a county road, in the hills, in a forest of stones.

I used to hunt in these trees and rocks. He seems really to want you to know that.

I used to hike this same trail. Alone, sometimes.

So this is not a just bizarre place where he intends, *may* harm you.

One handcuff dangles and jangles as you walk. He has not fastened both hands together, but has not taken the cuffs off.

You do not look for a way to break away from him, because you know he could run you down and you might even win the fight, but you are already winning *this* way, or at least, everything is all suspended, yes, suspended.

He walks alongside you, he does not even keep a few steps behind you. You are two people taking a cold, moonlight walk on the snow in each other's company. He seems to see it that way. That's what you want. And then you want to be able to walk away. If not that, he will take you somewhere else.

What did you hunt?

Bear. The way he laughs makes you think he would seem a charming man to unwary, trusting women. He gained the confidence of the other confident women, the police say— the FBI profilers. But don't worry, I'll protect you. You can't see whether he is sneering. Wildcats, too. Sorry, no snow snakes. Alligators though.

He holds up one of his boots to show the alligator skin.

He kicks the dirt and throws rocks when he talks, and when you say certain things, he shrugs his shoulders or comes to a full stop. Ask yourself why, and watch.

I like to fish, though.

Yeah? Me, too.

He stumbles a little on a root. Watch your step.

This is no place for high heels, but you walk as gracefully as you can, not vivaciously.

He keeps looking at you, as if he enjoys being with you, not as a man who will attack you at any moment. You are handcuffed together, as if holding hands.

Naked, Carol stepped up to her mother's antique tub, salvaged from one of the "cottages"—mansions—that burned on one of the little islands. "No, Lady, you have no way to step into a tub, so I won't either."

An hour after Carol was in bed, Jack came in dead tired, having been made a member of the search party, he said—out on the ice, among the islands, searching for the seventh young woman.

Jack's changed *his* MO, too. A searcher now, no less.

Even so, he was still cynical about the possibility of a catching "the Daylight Serial Killer."

Is the fox leading the chase? No woman in Watertown or Alexandria Bay can keep from wondering. Just as no woman can help but be watchful, wary.

After Jack fell asleep, Carol got up, drawn to the window overlooking the bay—her lifelong view of fabled Boldt Castle, fully lit, on Heart Island.

And you, Lady, are coming within view of Singer Castle on Dark Island.

I've never walked in the woods with a woman before, not even in the daytime.

You chose a good place for it.

Do you need to rest a while?

Could we?

No problem.

Let's look for a good place to sit.

There's that big house I remembered, out there.

He cuffs your hand to his hand. You are handcuffed together, as if holding hands.

He takes you back to the truck.

He parks the truck behind a deserted stone house, in a corner that blocks the view from the sharply curving road.

Part of the floor of the stone house has caved in, its planks pulled up, exposing the earth, black from campfires. Watching him start a fire, you see, imagine, him here other times.

You do not tremble, having a sure sense that he has brought you here only to be here with you and talk, or not talk. He suspects that when he talks he may lose his hold on you. But he craves hearing *you* talk. You control your usual vivacious way of talking, so not to overwhelm him.

Both of you are amazed that he has not forced anything, except at first, muscling you into his pickup, and maybe you have made him forget even that.

You let the night silence of the bay and its hills sink in. You do not call his attention to the sight through the trees of Singer Castle on Dark Island.

Lying on her back, her elbows supporting her uplifted, limp hands, thumbs, and forefingers lightly touching to frame the image, Carol watched the lady appear suddenly at the platform, go up the steps, and stand and look out over Lake Ontario, listen to the ice breaking up, and then start down again, again and again, even after she couldn't keep her eyes open any longer.

You wake up—first light glaring off the snow outside—in the stone house.

You've made it through one night, Lady.

You watch him stir, then wake up. You know he knows he could be in his warm bed in what the profiler on TV says is probably a comfortable house in a middle-class neighborhood.

He looks at you. He can't turn his head away from that smile.

All night—even dreaming—and all morning long, I have imagined it every which way, so that I can go with you, talk to you, and I *have* been with you, ever since that first moment I saw you, even the moment he took you, the moment I missed, imagined.

His nostrils flare suddenly, as if he is remembering things.

Keep quiet, keep still. It will pass, whatever it is.

Tim passed Carole's bedroom door.

"Wait a second, Tim. Do you hear that sound?"

"What sound?" Tim stood in the hall just outside the bedroom.

"Listen. . . . That sound. Ticking sound."

"Mother, that's icicles melting."

"But it's so loud."

If his nostrils flare like that after you say something, just say something very positive, or make some charming gesture to distract him.

And his eyes and that mouth. What do they tell you about him at any given moment? Like now, that look he just gave you.

I hope you didn't say something that sparked that look. Or is he remembering? Or did something just come over him that mystifies him?

Toast melting in her mouth, she realized that this was the first Sunday of the month and that in ten minutes or so the sacrament of the Lord's Supper would begin.

"I'm going to church."

Alone.

"Alone."

They're looking at me. Strange behavior. Service will be almost over. But there's still Communion, and that's really what I want.

Carol walked alone in a gentle swirling of snow, over uneven dirty ice, past Saint Cyril's Catholic Church, dark like a hillside fortress, her childhood fear of it lingering still.

You are aware that you are the eighth to get taken, the seventh one not yet found. You are remembering that the rapist dumped his first victim in Thompson Park, near the zoo, in Watertown six years ago, you remember the

16

TV newscasts about the discovery of the second victim in Alexandria Bay among the rocks in Keewaydin State Park, then the third victim, the fourth victim, the fifth victim, the sixth victim discovered on six islands in the Thousand Islands, all young women from Watertown, even though he took the sixth young woman from Alexandria Bay while she was visiting her grandmother here, and all were linked by MO and DNA to the same unidentified suspect.

But I feel it in my bones, Lady, that you will be the only woman who will escape and be found alive.

Climbing the Church Street hill past the grim, former jail building, Carol watched her church on Rock Street come, steeple to door to steps, into view. At the end of the long block, before she turned left, she envisioned the rock outcropping in the basement of her church, Alexandria Bay United Methodist, built 130-something years ago on Rock Street across from the stark Dutch Reformed Church, with whom the two now combined some activities.

Looking up at the Methodist steeple, she felt drawn to that basement rock, hearing her mother's voice explaining to her when she was six or so that the foundation of the church was cut into a single solitary immense stone. Secretly, she had sought it, along passageways, through doors, and seeing it, rushed toward it, upon it, touched it with both palms, hungering.

Taken later with her class to look upon the rock in the dank basement as a Sunday-school demonstration of what Jesus meant when he renamed Simon, Peter, the rock, on whom he built his Church, Carol had felt in her bones, I know, I know.

She imagined a voice saying, Rumor has it that Carol Helvy Seabold's new career change goal is to become an historian.

The greeter—Mrs. What's-her-name—was nicely surprised. "Good morning, Carol. Glad to see you back."

After missing six months of Sundays in a row.

Carol stood at the back.

Joan Blackwell was at the left-hand pulpit, this Sunday's reader. "A reading of the word of the Lord. Luke 19:40, 'I tell you that, if these should hold their peace, the stones would immediately cry out.'" As if she knew I was coming, what was on my mind.

How do they do it? Preachers. They always choose verses that apply to your own life, no matter what.

Lady, I must be with you, I will be with you, where you are, right this instant. I will it. So do not be afraid. I am with you every single moment. Like a movie in my head, a video, I can hit PAUSE, but don't worry, it won't be for long at a time.

Now, she was acutely aware, under the pew she shared with neighbors—of the rock. The rock among so many, very many such rocks in this region. "As many rocks in Alexandria Bay Village as there are islands in the Saint Lawrence River," her mother once whimsically estimated.

Is it the rock or the ritual that draws *me* back, that *I* hunger for? The rock the church rises upon or the ritual conducted between the rock and the steeple spire? Or both, in some odd combination she felt no need to verbalize?

You will survive. You *will* survive. You have the *will* to survive. They will find you in time.

No, you will suddenly appear on your own. You do not need those men zooming over the ice, searching among 1,800 islands to find that seventh young woman and now you, too. But you are not like the other women. You will not be discovered on an island in a luxurious summer cottage or mansion, propped upright, displayed in an easy chair. You will overcome him, or you will persuade him to let you go.

They missed me, my brothers and sisters. They aren't asking me why I have been away. They don't pry. They are good people. I miss them, too, Lady. I miss, through them, that sense of the Holy Spirit in this place.

Listening to Pastor Fredrika Sensibar's first sermon, I thought, You are not Reverend Neilson, and I missed him so much that for a long time in this place, I had to try very hard to feel one with the body of Christ, my brethren, and failed.

For six months, she had stayed home, as if on indeterminate vacation, because one Sunday morning she had found the house of the Lord vacant, spiritless.

She was conscious of being more aware now of the polished hardwood walls and the warm, white-oak, curved pews, the ceiling's three apexes, the curved altar, the old Scripture pulpit on the left, the new sermon pulpit on the right, the mammoth organ at the back between the pulpits, the large old-timey Christ-head painting to the left, the stained-glass Civil War memorial window for the Grand Army of the Republic to the right, all, since infancy, as familiar as her mother's kitchen, now her own.

Just in time. Well, both of us. Because Reverend Fredrika Sensibar, having already preached at Redwood Methodist Church this morning, double duty, had just now arrived, stepping up to the Lord's Supper.

Yes, that's what I had to come for. "Ritual time," Reverend Sensibar often called it. "When we partake of the Lord's Supper the first Sunday of each month, it is as if we are there, at the last supper when He first spoke those words. May we be full of an awareness that as we hear those words, others are hearing them from church to church, house to house, state to state, time zone to time zone, throughout the world, from minute to minute, day to day, year to year, era to era, unbroken, forever and ever—a single breathing. Listening.

"In the same night in which he was betrayed, Our Lord took bread—" Reverend Sensibar turned to the table and took up the loaf and in one graceful motion pivoted toward the congregation "—and when he had given thanks, he broke it—" she broke the bread in two "—and gave it to his disciples, saying, 'Take, eat. This is my body, which is given for you. Do this in remembrance of me.' Likewise, after supper he took the cup"—she turned and took up the cup and turned again to Carol and her fellow Christians—"and when he had given thanks, he gave it to them, saying, 'Drink ye all of this, for this is my blood of the New Covenant, which is shed for you and for many, for the forgiveness of sins. Do this, as oft as ye shall drink it, in remembrance of me.'"

"Amen." We all speak together in a single voice, Lady.

Leaning forward, Reverend Sensibar said, as if for the first time, "In the Methodist Church, we use the ancient method of intinction, whereby you dip the bread lightly in the wine—" I like this woman "—so that you may partake of both elements at once."

Out of uniform, Frank was in an attitude of prayer. He does not see me looking at him.

Carol watched each familiar back rise and turn, watched each profile move sideways into the aisle as the ushers invited them to the table, row after row.

I love you all.

I wish I could.

She remembered seeing a yellow-rimmed hole in the snow. A pissing deer, or a coyote, or a bear pissing. But no footprints. Why had the snow not covered it over, too? Remembering seeing it below the porch of the defunct fog house sent a chill up her back and over her scalp again. Here, only a moment ago, did the man in the snow mask piss from the porch?

He senses now that you need to go. So he steps away.

You hope he cannot hear you go.

But you hear him, loud, aimed against the scaling wallpaper of that deserted stone house, and you can't help imagining that vicious weapon dangling small and vulnerable, pudgy.

You walked up to that observation platform like walking up to a place you owned. To make an inspection and give orders to the hired help. It was the way you did it. And the clothes you wore. The clothes you are wearing now. High heels in the snow, walking up to the lighthouse. Bizarre in that place, but with class. A stride, not a walk. Your profile, standing there, Lake Ontario before you. Not like a queen. No, like a real person, a very real person. You were so real. *Are.* Vital. Vigorous.

In the empty space beside her, Carol imagined her mother sitting. As a child, she'd always wanted her mother to sit with her, her father on one side, her mother on the other. But her mother sang in the choir. Even so, when her mother sang solo, Carol was proud almost to tears. "That's my mother," she said to her father more than once.

"Yes, I believe she is."

She often turned to whoever happened to be sitting on the side where she wanted her mother to be sitting. "That's my mother."

"Is that your mother? Isn't that nice?"

Then she would stand up until her mother sat down.

But that time her father told her to sit back down. she knew why. For almost a year, she had been feeling too tall, conspicuous.

Even after her father had set the jar of ashes on the mantle, she had ever after heard her mother's voice rising up out of the choir.

"Can you hear her, or is it just me?"

"No, I can hear her."

Carol was glad her father had lied. "In every lie, lies a fraction of truth." Did Father say that?

"Just you and me." Back then, Carol believed everything Father said.

Her father still lived in Watertown, maybe grading papers at this hour, with wine.

The picnics with her mother at the lighthouse, just the two of them, were always a summertime, weekday event. No ice breaking up, crying. She had never heard that until last evening.

Looking left at the folding door that led to the fellowship hall and to the toilets, Carol wondered whether other women here were suffering her need— oh, yes, they are, about half are turning their heads slightly left.

Reverend Sensibar's benediction verged on the cryptic. "Let this mind be in you which was also in Christ Jesus."

After church, her fingers on the ignition, her mother always declared, "I feel restored," in a musical voice.

Then her mother would have to go to work the next evening in Watertown, on the night shift, passing Carol's father's car as he was coming home, a briefcase full of student papers, tests.

The hospital odors were in her hair as her mother bent to kiss her awake, seeming to know Carol was only pretending to be asleep.

Then she would carry Carol into the kitchen, where her father was stirring up the fumes of breakfast.

When Carol got older, her mother called her to come to the table.

She always waited until her mother appeared in the bedroom doorway to open her eyes.

Her mother leaned against the doorjamb, kicking off her shoes, until Carol came to her, and they would walk hand in hand into the kitchen, mother's feet cooling on the cold floor.

"Now *there's* a pretty picture." Her father always stopped fixing eggs or griddle cakes to point his spatula at them as she and her mother came through the doorway.

But at the table and in the living room and all around the house and out on the front porch, they said very little, in motion or at rest, bodies, voiceless.

Carol rose with others in her row, stepped into the aisle, and led the others toward the altar.

Frank is looking at me. But he has liked me, from our Sunday-school years all the way through our high-school days. Not my voice, I hope. He is not just a small-town cop. He's a cop's cop. That time when we were kids, about nine, fiddle-fucking around. Did he seduce me, or me him? I forget.

Carol took the bread from Reverend Sensibar's hand and dipped it in the cup Kyle Breedon held out to her. Kneeling at the altar, she looked up at the cross, closed her eyes, pushed the bread between her lips. As she slowly chewed, she felt the Holy Spirit suffuse her body and mind, steeped in ritual time.

God, Abba, I pray it is your will that the stalwart lovely lady returns safe. Dear Jesus, I pray she is talking to you now. Holy Spirit, I pray you are comforting her in her trial, her tribulation.

Holy Spirit, I am not, I know, telling *the* story, but *a* story. It is *your* spirit who moves in *the* story. But I pray you will mingle your spirit with mine and hers, to save her. Even if she has died quickly as the others died, or even if she has already escaped, didn't our mingled spirits comfort her or help her to overcome? Amen.

Lady, I am with you always.

Snow falling, Carol walked over the ice downhill and over to Market Street, past the venerable old library building, converted into the Chamber of Commerce, to Dockside Pub, resenting these anchors in the actual.

Walking away from the dogsled race yesterday, reaching out to touch as she passed the blind woman who won, an impulse to go to the lighthouse had swept her uphill to the car, and off to the highway, Melissa, as always, buckled into the child restraint.

Aware of the OPEN YEAR ROUND sign in the window—big deal around here, so few places are—she entered the liveliness of Dockside Pub.

You turned with one vigorous motion and stepped off the platform, your rich brown leather purse hanging from a strap over your shoulder. *Yours.* *Your* purse. *Your* high-heeled shoes. *Your* successful career woman earth-brown winter coat. Tan skin. Athletic. Tennis. Not from lying in the sun or in a tanning bed. Jet black hair. Okay, dyed, maybe. Vital just standing there. Vital in motion. Decisive.

When she looked up at the doorway to watch people come in, bright light from the sun on the snow turned her neighbors into silhouettes.

In, as she expected, came Jack, then Melissa, then Tim. Searching for your missing cook? She asked Joan to bring a Saranac root beer for Tim, who once said he could taste its history, since 1888.

As her "family unit" sat down, Carol got up to go to the restroom.

The spoken word "missing" turned Carol around and back into the pub proper where she saw the lady's dark face, a glamorous photograph, "Glenda Hamilton" spelled out beneath it.

What gets my attention, Glenda—now, Lady, I can call you by name—is that you have that look about you that tells the world, I am *it,* I have done it, I can do more, too, watch me go, and don't distract me.

Then there she is on film, walking toward Carol in a business suit, coming out of some art gallery in Watertown.

"The fifty-six-year-old arts advocate was last seen getting into her burgundy Mercedes for the long drive to New York City to visit her husband, who is undergoing a series of treatments for lung cancer."

Police say you are not considered missing until twenty-four hours have passed.

"But that she left her car behind, however, raises concerns . . .

"If you have any information about Hamilton's whereabouts, you are urged to call police at 315-783-2283. You need not give your name."

Jack, Tim, and Melissa insisted that Carol walk "with the family" back home.

"Look! A wolf!" A woman leaving the Catholic church pointed toward Heart Island, Boldt Castle. In the wintertime, wolves, they say, get into the tower and make a lair of it.

Turning completely around in a circle on the ice-crusted sidewalk, Carol did not see a wolf.

"Where?" Jack wasn't even looking around.

Melissa stared as if she saw it.

"Out there on the ice, heading for Wellesley Island."

"We gonna see all kinds of critters out there now that the river's frozen over."

"And more bodies."

Tim slid on the sidewalk ice to Jack's side. "Maybe the wolves will gang up on him or coyotes or maybe somebody will mistake him for a deer and shoot him between the eyes."

In the house, talking to Glenda, Carol walked from room to room, avoiding Jack and Tim, winking when Melissa crossed her path.

Can I tell you a secret, something personal about myself?

I'm listening. But make it short.

Yes, now you can go to work on him, because now you feel he knows you are truthful, that you don't fake it with him.

Well, I told my daughters I was going to visit my husband in the hospital. It's a 360-mile, six-hour trip.

What you want to tell me a lie like that for?

You don't recognize me, do you?

Why *would* I recognize you?

Haven't you ever seen me on television?

Don't try to tell me you're some kind of a movie star.

No, on the news over the years, for this and that, but recently when I ran for Watertown city council, and sometimes in feature stories, and on public television. Now, do you know me?

Sure, I used to work in the art museum—as a sanitary engineer. Yeah.

You did? Small world, huh?

Well, just that one week. I tend to drift from one job to another.

Glenda, you don't want him to tell you too much personal information about himself.

Then you may know that my name is Glenda Hamilton, and that I am the wife of Dr. Denton Hamilton of Good Samaritan Hospital in Watertown.

You can call me F, for the highest grade I ever earned.

Sure, F. Well, I set out to visit my husband in the hospital in Manhattan. He has very serious, inoperable lung cancer and is undergoing the most powerful series of radiation treatments. Or that's what I told my daughters I was setting out to do. But I had a plan.

So did I.

He laughs.

Laugh with him.

Yes, we both had plans. Mine was to visit him one last time and then withdraw all the money from a secret account I have in a bank on Staten Island and just keep right on going—out of the country.

Let that sink in.

You can almost *hear* it sink in.

His face shows he believes you, but he is speechless.

A few minutes later, he is falling in with it.

They'll be looking for you at the hospital. Do they know you're coming? When was you supposed get there?

You need to worry he will see it in your eyes, if you lie.

Wednesday. I always take my time—visit my housebound aunt on my mother's side halfway, in Troy.

Yes. F believes you. You could have won awards for lying. You hope it hits him like a miracle—all that money, maybe to go to someplace like Venezuela, "The Gateway to South America," my mother once said, "Little Venice," my father one-upped her. Or the Amazon, or some such place else, even Greece, even Sweden, get away from all of them who are looking for him now. As far away as Outer Mongolia. But the thought of such money does not make him pant.

Did they move Manhattan to Canada?

I wanted Melissa to see the lighthouse where *my* mother took me on a picnic that time, just us, because this time next year, I may not *be* here. Tell F the same thing, Glenda.

I wanted to see the lighthouse where my mother took me on many picnics one last time. Shall we go to Staten Island?

A lint ball under the dining room table made Carol feel certain that lint balls lay under and behind every piece of furniture.

She saw herself down on her hands and knees, moving throughout the house, downstairs and up, inspecting.

Not to keep the house spotless, but to find out what things the house was keeping from her.

"This just in. This afternoon at three p.m., Police Chief Mitch Phillips announced that even though Glenda Hamilton is not yet officially a missing person, a search began just moments ago."

She walked into the family room, where, on Jack's theater-scale, family-budget-busting screen, she saw a picture-postcard view of Tibbetts Point Lighthouse in Spring time.

"The first twenty-four hours are critical."

Glenda, I want you to know that I do not accept the first twenty-four-hour rule.

"Because Tibbetts Point Lighthouse is located within about thirty miles of where the bodies of five of the six murdered women were found, the search has begun in that area.

"After searchers found the fifth body in January on Heart Island, a small island in the Saint Lawrence River at Alexandria Bay accessible by ice, the police, expecting that the killer would eventually leave another body on that island, searched Boldt Castle's six stories and one hundred and twenty rooms, and found nothing."

"Ask me, and I'd say they're still over there, lying in wait for him, hoping he'll think they're all gone now."

Tim happened into the room when Jack said that. "Dad, how do you know these things?"

"I'm your father, son, that's how."

"A black pickup, about ten years old, make and model unknown, covered with snow, was seen speeding away from the scene, reported by an anonymous caller. Preliminary forensic examination of the Hamilton Mercedes has revealed nothing to indicate foul play, much less any connection with the murders of the six young women, three of which have been linked so far by DNA to the same unknown male. A search has already been under way for a seventh missing woman, Kathy Donovan, also of Watertown."

Would they some evening report that an anonymous, rather nondescript woman was seen standing huddled up against Tibbetts Point Lighthouse, hugging her six-year-old, sucking on a broken kaleidoscope cut in her thumb, on the edge of nowhere?

They are showing you giving a speech when you ran for the city council last year.

They showed the chief full figure, Boldt Castle tower over his shoulder. "We think maybe what he does, he walks or drives a truck across the ice to an island and leaves the body inside the cottage and covers his tracks somehow, going out and coming back." He spoke in a high-pitched monotone, looking up, as if scolding somebody in an attic above him. "Or the snow does it for him. That's how we have a little bit of trouble finding his victims. We have almost a hundred snowmobiles, ice boats, power sleds, what have you, hovercrafts, Polarises out there, including some folks from the snow mobile rally and some folks from the Thousand Islands Sled Dog River Run. And we approach each island, each cottage with great caution, because we don't know how long he stays with his victims."

The self-confident young red-haired woman anchor seemed to be broadcasting an affinity for Glenda. "Glenda Hamilton is well known and respected as an arts and preservation activist who ran in a hotly contested race for city council last year and lost by only a few votes.

"A former high-school art teacher, Hamilton has served on numerous boards as a civic leader and won many awards on city, state, and national levels. Hamilton is the wife of Dr. Denton Hamilton, a surgeon at Good Samaritan Hospital in Watertown, who is being treated for lung cancer in a Manhattan hospital."

The chief came back on, only a talking, sleepy-eyed head now. "The search is only a precautionary measure. At this juncture, we have little or no reason to conclude a crime has been committed. We join the family in hoping that Glenda Hamilton will return safe and sound."

So now, I know where I saw you before, on TV a lot, saw that same confident, vigorous walk. I knew it, watching you doing good work and getting honored for it, a successful career woman. Wife of a doctor. Rich probably. The police spokeswoman at the microphones reported your age as fifty-six. And then there—in the photograph your daughter Paulette held up—was that smile I had already imagined.

And that smile in the photographs she showed would make anybody think you—no matter how old you are—know how to talk to people and win them over to your side in any situation.

And you are certain that you are going to get out of *this* situation. Because your daughter's words are the words for what I saw when I was watching you. Only for a few minutes.

It's on his mind too. You an executive? Those clothes you wearing.

I've been involved in the arts all my life.

Born artist, huh?

I began professionally when I was twenty-one as an educator in the arts. What were you doing when *you* were twenty-one?

None of your business. His tone has shifted to wary. What do you do as an educator? Principal? Whipping kids' asses?

I'm a painter, but I get involved in various projects having to do with all the arts and with preservation. Before I retired, I was a high school art teacher.

So, you been correcting my grammar in your head the whole time, like *all* teachers.

You haven't talked that much.

I *don't* talk much. I can tell jokes okay, I guess. Seems there was this stranger from Mississippi, tourist, driving between Clayton and Cape Vincent, sees big, flat area covered with snow, asks this man walking along the road, What all kind of stuff do you all grow in that there field? Man looks where the driver's pointing, says, Lake Ontario.

That *is* funny.

I can eat, too, if I had something to eat.

Me, too. Coffee, anyway. I—

Carol's father, suddenly appearing in the doorway, interrupted.

Why did Father bring his briefcase into the house, and it Sunday, too?

So I would know who he is?

Even sets it right by his foot. The same foot that kicked in the front door the night he lost his keys.

Misplaced them, as it turned out.

Oh, they'll turn up sooner or later.

Coming home, off her shift, her mother had given the busted door a little push with the toe of her white nurse's shoes.

Meanwhile, how do we keep robbers out of my house? To remind him that she had bought the house with her own money before she married him.

"Remember the time you kicked in the front door?"

"Remember the time I did what?"

"Kicked in the front door."

"What is your mother talking about, Melissa?"

"The time you kicked in the front door, Grandfather."

"Your daughter is a bright one."

"Skip it."

Glenda, I think I'll come right out and ask my father whether he has any ongoing secrets.

Father, do you have any ongoing secrets? Is your past dark, Father?

Maybe I'll ask him tomorrow or the next day.

Maybe never.

"Daddy, I'm dying to know . . ."

"What?"

"Nothing."

"No, what, what?"

"No, I was just wondering whether you put both socks on before you put on each shoe, or whether you do a sock and a shoe, a sock and a shoe."

"I'm a psychologist, daughter, not a theologian."

"Your socks don't match, Grandfather."

But the main point, Glenda, is that there Father sits, and has been sitting longer than usual. As if he *needs* to come over here, after class or office hours, and sit with us, rarely though it is, and even though today is only Sunday—for some reason, or no reason. I guess love means not having to say anything.

"You know what Jack calls this village?"

"Yes." Her father seemed delighted she'd asked that question.

"Shitsville."

"And with variations. Such as Shitsburg. I once said to him, 'Well, Jack, if you think *you're* too good for this town, then it must be worse than you think.'"

"Did he laugh?"

"Didn't laugh."

"Did he even get it?"

"Don't think he did."

"Jack said he once aspired to something higher."

"Did you ask him, 'Do you think of yourself as a multitude of one, or as one of a multitude?'"

No, but I will.

Realizing that she had not really noticed Gordon's birch tree lately, she deliberately looked out the window at it. Late one night, as a surprise, before they got married, Gordon planted a tree in her mother's yard, and she had watched it grow. A positive image for twelve years, even after the divorce and she married Jack. After the great ice storm last winter, it seemed to die. But her father trimmed it and the tree revived in the spring.

"Father, do you think Gordon's tree will come out this year?"

"Yes."

"No." Melissa pretended to be contrary.

Maybe.

You've got to admit, Glenda. This is very odd. My father comes and sits for what is a very long time for him and then leaves when Jack's mother and father come in the door from their retirement cottage in Clayton on one of their rare visits, without an occasion for an excuse.

And now there *they* sit. Distractions.

She rummaged around in her mind for questions and comments that have something to do with housekeeping so her mother-in-law will not feel such a stranger and for something to ask or say about life insurance to make her father-in-law feel welcome.

Not that I think I am too good to talk to them, Glenda, but that I would rather be talking exclusively to you.

"Mother Seabold, I saw Crystal Light on sale, two for one, at the Big M."

"I betcha *our* Big M in Clayton is bigger than *your* Big M. Ha. Ha."

Father Seabold always knew when his wife would offer no reply.

"Do you miss the insurance business, Father Seabold, now that you are retired?"

"Him retired? Not on your life. Him retired?" Mother Seabold set herself off bouncing in silent, feigned laughter. "He's still in it, up to his eyebrows."

"My mother worked almost every day or night of her life." She saw her mother in white, walking down an endless corridor, green as water.

"I couldn't live the way your poor mother did."

Mother couldn't either.

Using both hands, Father Seabold scraped his bald pate decisively.

"I like to keep my hand in."

"See my toy?" Melissa knew the effect of such a question from past visits. "It's broken, but it's still beautiful if you hold it against the light, just right. See my wound?" She ripped off the soiled Band-Aid.

Now all I need is for my brother Jason to show up, just passing through, from somewhere—stops, just like Jack, at the refrigerator, sticks his head inside, looks at almost everything in it before he backs up, straightens up, slams the

29

door, just as he did all through his teenage years, disappointed—on his way down to Buffalo. Same-o, same-o, he always says, to make contact with our common past.

You know, I try very hard, I really try to make contact with Jason's wife, on her rare visits, and might succeed if Faye would stop talking. Well, she does, if Father walks into the room, knowing he will ask her what she means, exactly, every other sentence she utters.

Faye showed up the day I returned home from surgery, as if Jason had sent her ahead as his representative, and next morning, Jason himself showed up, kissed my cheek, told me, "You gonna be fine," then sat beside Jack in front of Jack's theater-sized TV for the endless overtime game between the greatest this one and the greatest that one. "We gonna have to go, Carol," was one of his longest speeches.

Bye.

Jack came in, said hello mom, hello dad, dad do you want a cold beer, yes son, believe I do, went to the refrigerator, came back with a cold beer (there being hardly any such thing as a hot beer), caught himself, asked, mom, and you? nothing for me, dear, came back armed with two beer bottles, held down by the neck as if about to toss World War I grenades like the ones his old fishing buddy Hobart used to collect, "murdered," Jack said, by friendly fire in Iraq last month, sat down.

I'm certain if you were a guest here, Glenda, you could get us all to talking to each other, and, starting with your warm elegant gestures and laying on of hands, even get us to touching as we talk.

Carol felt the house go empty, as it was before she was born, when Wayne Harrington broke in, his vacant home place, and slept on the floor in the sleeping bag before his wife came knocking at the door, a surprise.

He's in the house, now—his finger on the trigger, those few minutes of his future ahead of him.

Melissa looked all around, as if she had read Carol's mind.

Tim came in and sat down.

Carol stood up and sat right back down, blushing, and Glenda kicks in the door. "I'm back."

My last picture of you was you stepping off the observation platform as if over a threshold, and that was when my six-year-old distracted me, like I told you before.

Why, I do not remember.

You have this aura that's kept him from even touching you. He is probably not much older than your oldest daughter and you have so confused him by being older than the other women but beautiful from a distance and in the twilight snow light by the lighthouse. He hesitated too long, giving you time to talk, sensible talk, but charming in the *way* you talk.

I suppose why I jumped in the car and shot off in pursuit, once I realized you must have been taken, was because when I was seventeen, I was standing at a truck stop on Highway 12 with the kids I ran with, and I happened to look up out of our circle at a huge semi truck pulling out onto the highway, and heard a girl's voice yell, Help me! and strained to hear it again, but didn't, so I turned and asked the others if they heard somebody yell from the truck, but they all said no, but I was sure, even so, I didn't say anything, didn't do anything, but I never forgot the way hearing that voice made me feel. So, do you suppose that was it? What started me off after his pickup truck?

"Who took my Greek washcloth?" Her only memento from the winter she crossed northern Greece solo on her bicycle to prove to herself that she was not by nature vulnerable.

Nobody answered.

"God is in the details." Tim's latest all-occasion toss-off line triggered a response this time.

"Not in all of them."

Such as coming into a room where Jack has just left a smell even a dog would not inflict, or Jack comes into the kitchen, which the world supposes is my domain, and cuts loose as if I am not there. I know we are married eleven years and all that. But even so. I always get up and leave the room when *I* feel the urge.

He does it in the truck and you laugh and do it too because you have held it in until it's just too painful and maybe he has too and you're lucky that he laughs too. It could have made him mad, you laughing. I don't think it's funny. But I am here to help you stay alive, so whatever you have to do, do it.

She saw herself assembling her bike in the Athens airport and in the dead of winter setting out across Greece, with very few things in her panniers, and on to Venice and Rome. Even though she had escaped sixteen years ago from under the brandished baton of a blind date's half-erect penis, his very attempt was so traumatic she had known she had to take control of her life in some fearless act. Taking pictures only in her head, all dim now, along with her self-confidence. Watching that young blond photographer looking compassionately at, and then focusing in on, an old lady, a black, fringed shawl over her head, a large wicker basket of pears in her spread lap, and before she could speak to him, he leapt on his bicycle and was far ahead of her before she could follow.

No one ever knew—except my lover James years later—about that event, that trip, this aftermath.

I am an eyewitness, but all I saw of him was his snow mask and his black pickup truck, parked ahead of my car and yours. The news said it was a white pickup, reported by somebody else who also said she saw it, speeding out of Clayton. So I am not telling you I *saw* him grab you and witnessed your struggle. I heard no scream, but then you would not have screamed, not you, you would just have struggled fiercely or known not to resist the gun pointed at your head or the knife at your throat. But they say, do not, do not, above all, *do not* ever, *ever* get in the car with them.

My husband's trying to get in from behind. Sneaky, aren't they? Don't they know they will wake you every time? Like just now. Unless you're drunk, which I was that one time only. When I realized I not only didn't remember what I had done that night, but imagined what might have been done to me— one of the few parties I went to when I was a freshman at Syracuse—it turned me off drinking much. You being drunk gives them the idea they can come in from behind and you won't even know it. And they get that idea from when you pretend to be asleep because you don't want to get involved. The way I'm doing now. Is it the pussy or the sneakiness that appeals to them most? And why in the middle of the night? Near miss in a wet dream?

She recalled Jack crawling into bed on their first night smelling of wood shavings, oiled tools, eye-stinging glue, and marine paint, masking any sweat, and his breath smelled of the Wild Turkey Carol had sipped with him. "Promise me, you will tell me if it hurts." He was as shy coming into her as when she had noticed him coming into Dockside Pub that first sight of him.

Shyness shot with steel, Glenda, a quiet man who puts things together to make a boat all day long appealed to a young woman who had come apart, bit by bit over two years. I remember only vaguely the way he was, this man that I see, hear, smell, and taste so vividly now.

What irritates me tonight is not him fumbling back there—not *into* my behind, Glenda, only with James that one time, experimenting—but the fact that I will not be with you. Not being fully awake—and it three in the a.m.—I can't control my thoughts of you, and so things could go wrong now for you more easily.

Carol turned to him and took his cock into her hand, disdain mingling with pleasure anticipated.

BRIDGE FREEZES FIRST.

There's a shabby little summer cottage FOR RENT up ahead.

He will break in through the back door. Furnished—twin beds like a motel setup. Good. Good. But only if . . .

Fear strikes you, like your husband suddenly realizing he must die. Imagine you have gone home, to your childhood home. Yes, do that when fear strikes, or be an alien from some far-off country without a name, that none of this, not even the lighthouse and the ice on the lake, has ever been in your life.

Do not let him see that night sweat, Glenda. It will remind him of how you two came to be in the same room.

I am an eyewitness, but except for what I told Frank, as an anonymous person on the phone, I am no help to Jack and the other men bouncing over the ice among the islands in an off-key chorus of revving motors and airboat fans, looking for two women now. No help to the police spokeswoman standing stiff and at a loss for words before the local and network microphones.

But I *am* a witness for you, Glenda, to help keep you alive—talking to you, thinking positive thoughts, with what I see you do and say.

Not that you desperately need my help, *any* help. Because watching you, what I still feel in my bones is how on top of the world you looked, even there at the end of the earth on the lake. How you could out talk anyone. How you could even overpower anyone. I have faith in you, and I have faith, I pray, and that's power, too. Not to ask God to change His plan—if He *has* one. I am only helping God keep you in mind. The story I am imagining may not actually be your story, but any story that keeps you alive will somehow, in the realm of the spirit, help you.

Not my thoughts exactly. The images. Like a movie. I see you like you are in this movie. You're the star, and he, whoever he is, is, of course, the villain. Some villain. Well, he did do what he did to the others. But they weren't *you.* Vital. Vigorous. I see you talking him out of it. I even see you persuading him to surrender and face the consequences. If not, I see you overpowering him. You think, If I can just get behind him when he nods off like that, I can throw my handcuffs over his head and choke him. Vital. Vigorous.

He has met his match.

2

Popping a sheet warm from the dryer into a white belly shape high over the bare mattress, watching it float down, deflating, Carol saw Glenda rise from a twisted sheet and swing her long legs over the edge of a twin bed, first in her own home, again in the stone cottage F invaded.

We— You made it through another night. I hope me thinking about you, talking to you, seeing you much of the night and all day helped.

You are still talking to him.

He says nothing about it, but maybe he saw you on TV too, doing the many things you do, but has not yet really recognized you. Several different photographs of you, too, on the news over those six years, formal and candid, as who you are, a confident career woman. He surely watched that relentless coverage of the seven women, and watched your story unfold year by year as he watched his own. To him, it is his story, not each of the women's. He got to see them over and over, even after he finished with them. And saw drawings of himself as a man from Mars, because nobody could look like those drawings. Did it make him mad not to see himself up there as he really is, when the women were shown just as they were, looking their best? Was that even his model of pickup truck they showed an example of every night? Reported it first a few years ago as a white SUV with a red streak on the front bumper— makes me think, yeah, hit and run.

It must be weird to him to be on the news every single solitary day and night and not recognize yourself the way they show you and the way they talk about you. If you see this man, call the police. Do not approach him. He is armed and dangerous. A family member may notice a change in habits or routine. He may criticize the police's methods of investigation. They keep coming up with tips.

He probably thought, that's not even vaguely me they are talking about, but it definitely was me who took her and her and her and her and her and her. They don't say eight, because they don't officially include you yet.

I need to focus. For *your* sake.

You see that his hands are still stained from some kind of work—boats, trains, trucks.

He keeps looking at *your* hands, which are large for a woman, veined.

If you could get at him, you could choke him to death with those hands. Maybe he suspects that. You naturally touch people with those hands when you talk to them, maybe too much. One friend told you, friend to friend, Glenda, you touch people too often. Men may misunderstand. But one man said you were charming because you reach out and touch people so naturally to stress a point.

You see he's been pondering something. Wait. He will say.

That was a Mercedes you were driving, right?

Yes.

I wasn't sure, what with the snow coming down the way it was. So I guess there's more where that came from.

Exactly three hundred thousand. Plus interest.

He stands up and looks down at you. What you trying to say?

I'm inviting you to go with me to make that withdrawal.

F walks around, looking into the landscape painting (same as the one up in Mother's attic) hanging cockeyed on the wall between the twin beds, then at you, and walks around some more.

What about your husband?

I wouldn't mind skipping the visit. It's the long drives and the visits—especially the visits—that I do not want to endure anymore. We would make compatible traveling companions. You have been a perfect gentleman.

Almost too thick. But he seems to beam in the morning light.

F trusts you.

But he's like a pit bull. No telling what might set him off, at your throat.

The profiler on TV always says he is very intelligent and plans everything in advance and has anticipated all contingencies in every circumstance.

You heard that, too, even as you were watching the news about your own activities, those shots of you running for office, the TV promos and reports on cultural events, smiling, with that look you have. I didn't consciously recognize you when I watched you at the lighthouse, but you had a sort of glow about you, a woman who had faced situations with courage, grace, and determination to keep yourself intact.

Frank's patrol car passed Carol's house for the second time this morning.

Carol woke Melissa. "Thirsty for a slurpie, kid?"

"It's not summertime."

"Okay, a smoothie."

"Awesome. But what about my test? I can add but I still can't subtract."

My town is stone and brick buildings, and some houses are stone and some stand right by huge rocks that you could reach out through your window and touch.

Melissa slurping a smoothie in the backseat, Carol wondered where they could go, decided on Ogdensburg, over the bridge into Canada and then east about forty miles, in the vicinity of where Glenda and F might be hiding.

"Rapid transit, rapid transit, rapid transit."

"What in the world are you saying there in the backseat?"

"Rapid transit, rapid transit, rapid transit."

"Yes, I know, but why?"

"I like the sound of it."

"You're going to be a poet."

"Maybe yes, maybe no."

No, the public library, Ogdensburg later.

When she looked up from the computer, where she was about "to get the hang of this thing," and around it for a view across the lobby of the children's library, the sloppily fat reference librarian was sitting on one of the little red chairs, bent down, seeming to be whispering to Melissa.

Carol, you had better— Glenda's voice, a former teacher's admonitory tone.

"What was that man saying to you?"

"Nothing."

"It didn't look like nothing to me. Haven't I told you time and time again not to—"

"But he's not a stranger. He's the library man."

A new one.

"Thanks, Roland." The regular children's librarian seemed to be coming back from the restroom, looking a little nervous. Carol suspected she saw the look on Carol's face as she looked at the reference librarian.

Now Sir Roland is leering at that middle-aged woman's ass. I have wronged him. His friendliness toward Melissa was innocent.

She wanted to apologize, but in the nature of things she'd have to tell a long, awkward story.

But what I felt then was certainly real, Glenda. And now this feeling that the situation was wrong is also real. Now I am thinking as my father thinks. But I have no idea whether he cares that I am thinking as he thinks.

Any more than my mother really cared whether I became a nurse like her or not.

Think your own thoughts, Carol.

Carol remembered when she was nine and Jason was five, the time she just wanted to touch it. Pure curiosity. That one time only, but her mother, still in her head nurse uniform, caught her. "It's only natural. But don't do it again—if you can help it."

She had not thought of holding a mirror up to her vagina to see what Bill had seen, until she and Peggy agreed to open themselves up to each other. Pure curiosity.

That was all, Glenda. Did you ever do like that? Frankly, we also touched each other's nipples. Just to see what it felt like. Other girls went further. Some went all the way. But with boys, too. Most of them, it seemed to me.

Does Tim then ever mess around with Melissa? Oh, I hope not. Natural or not.

I must be more vigilant.

But do I want to walk in on it? And what about Tim and his pal, Logan, who hates sports?

Stereotypes, Carol, are a form of terrorism.

You sound like my father.

In fact, my father should be in on this. He might shed some light on it all. Then again, he might toss it off with a psychology department witticism or sarcasm. Or clam up, the way he mostly is, when not holding forth before hundreds.

Everywhere I go, people are talking about the Daylight Killer, and that he has taken another woman from Watertown, but for women here in Alexandria Bay, too, to be on our guard.

Wanting on impulse to talk with Frank, she walked across the common parking area to a large modern building that housed the city hall, the fire department, and the police station. On the side, the small door that led to the cramped office of the police department was locked. OUT SICK.

But there was Frank in Dockside Pub, his head bent over a bowl of steaming soup.

"Eating that good old homemade soup, I see."

"Chowder. Have to, on that. Bad cold. Fluids. Stand back."

She sat behind him, back to back, ordered bowls of chowder for herself and Melissa, and, half turned around, talked to Frank's back. "The news said you were called to Tibbetts Point Lighthouse that night."

"Yeah, that was me." He didn't even turn his head. "And that was you, but don't you worry. On that."

She absorbed the silence.

"Melissa had never seen Tibbetts Point Lighthouse before."

"So now she has."

That's it?

When he finished, he stood up, but still didn't turn. "See you in church, Carol."

The sound of her name coming out of Frank's mouth had always made her feel safe.

* * *

Carol listened again to a week-old message on the voice recorder. "Dr. Christina Trenton asked me to call you to remind you of your appointment, seven a.m. Monday, March eighth, for the follow-up surgery."

Carol hit "delete."

That hip-hop star—what's-her-name, bless her heart—showed her scar—just short of the nipple—on the *Tonight* show to scare us all into getting mammograms.

To escape the voice recorder, she stepped out on the front porch, sucked in the icy air.

Seeing Mrs. Webb waving through the part in her curtains, Carol remembered what she had told her as she and Melissa had been getting into the car to go to the lighthouse.

"Mrs. Seabold, I saw a coyote on your rooftree this morning."

"Oh, no, Mrs. Webb, that must have been our big cat."

"Oh, no, Mrs. Seabold. You might want to keep your eye out for it."

Tim came in, trailing Logan.

"My mother wanted me to ask you what your profession is, Mrs. Seabold."

"Well, Logan, I am studying to become a nurse, perhaps beyond that to become a doctor. And what is it your mother . . . ?"

"She's a systems manager."

"I see."

"I wish *I* did. What *is* a systems manager?"

"'Fraid you'll have to ask your mother, Logan."

"I did. She said it was too complicated to explain and she had to run."

"Busy lady. Well, you do know what a nurse does, don't you?"

"Oh, Mom, Logan wasn't born yesterday."

"Well, Logan, did you know that it is a fact around here that an island is not counted as an island among the eighteen hundred and seventy-two islands of the Thousand Islands unless it has at least two trees?"

"Yes."

"The two of you are too smart for me."

Amiably, they raised their eyebrows and rolled their eyes and turned into Tim's room.

Somehow disturbed by the fact that an island is not counted as an island unless two trees grow on it, she had rowed out last spring to an island she had chosen a few years before, finally to plant a tree to rise up and stand beside the lone tree already standing there when she was born, in view through her mother's bird-watching binoculars from the upstairs east window. Snow covered it now, but in April, she intended to row out there, and hoped to see a vigorous sprout.

She pulled out her latest assignment in her correspondence course in nursing. Two weeks late.

"Nurse? Nurse? When are you going to begin to nurse your own husband, as it were?" Jack stood stock still that night, a Bud in one hand, a Lucky Strike in the other, a false look on his face.

The lesson asked Carol, "If you press the skin on a patient's leg and you leave your thumbprint, what is presented?"

Worried that she would never finish this correspondence course, she pressed her thumb into her own leg, leaving no impression. The lesson nearly finished, she set it aside.

When you are terminally ill, they will take you out on the ice and "leave you to your own devices."

Certain that Melissa was not faking sleep, her after-lunch nap, Discovery Channel still turned low on her little battery-operated TV, images of the Pine Barrens of New Jersey flashing, Carol was about to go into the front room to surf the seemingly thousand channels to watch something, dreading the tedious, usually fruitless search—but first a stop in the bathroom—when she heard a newscaster's unnatural voice introduce the policewoman spokesperson for the Watertown police department, who updated the public on TV morning, noon, and evening, and just again before bedtime, about the Daylight Serial Killer, as they called him, and his victims.

She keeps stressing that the first twenty-four hours are critical. Well, I stand here to stress to you that I do not accept the twenty-four-hour rule. Even though this is the third day.

You should see those men—Jack among them now—but led by a woman, Thyre Mann, the forensic anthropologist called in from Buffalo, who'd led the search for bodies, after she was the one who found the third one. Frantically looking for you now, like they looked for each of the seven before, but the search for you seems more frantic than for each of the others. Because of who you are, important, not just in Watertown, in the state, too.

They say, they say what they say, but I say he is a white man of about thirty-five, very intelligent, and you are in a rusty black pickup truck—except of course when it snows like it was that evening and like it is doing now outside my window—according to us two witnesses, that other woman and me.

What matters is that you are alive, miles away from the Thousand Islands, or you would be found. They go over and over and over the earlier cases of the six women whose bodies were found, show their pictures, all of them lovely and lively, and tell their stories, and their mothers or husbands or sisters and brothers come on, demanding that the task force catch the killer.

The FBI and the state and local agencies are working together "tirelessly" to bring this "gentleman" to justice. I cringe every time I hear them call him "gentleman." "The woman" is what they call us when we rob or kill, not "lady." But if you call him "gentleman," you have a reason to. If the Daylight Serial Killer is a gentleman, what kind of person is not? He's on a killing "spree," they say, like women on a shopping spree. And they say, we'll all breathe "a little bit easier" when he's caught. Merely "a little bit"? Words fail.

I personally am not afraid anymore because you two are long gone somewhere into a maze of back roads to dodge police cars. Unless there are others where *he* came from. Yes, I guess there are. Always *is*.

Men looking for *the* man, a woman in uniform telling us what the men are doing, and that the fact of the day is that they have found nothing to lead them to the man. Why a man? It is always a man, like it's a fact of nature or something. Why do they never consider a woman, I wonder? It could be a woman abducting a woman. Women stalk men and rob Stop 'N' Gos and kill their children and stab their sleeping husbands, don't they? The car they found at the scene is a Mercedes, your car, so you have that much money, and so, could be that a *woman* needs money, not just a man. To start a new life somewhere else. F wants more than money from you.

But they are not even admitting that the man you are with is the Daylight Serial Killer because they found no DNA at the lighthouse to link him to the other six women. They are convinced the seventh woman is a victim. But you are only a missing person, they say. But not in my mind. I know what no one else knows.

I just realized something about myself. I cannot just sit down and name off all the women. Sometimes two, but not all seven in a row. Maybe because the TV newscasters always go to the same two mothers for a reaction when the task force announces something—or nothing. "Nothing" makes this one mother call for a demonstration on the steps of the courthouse. "The city hall on Washington Street is the asshole of the universe." That's my husband talking, and even my son, behind my back, repeats it to his friends. Tim has many friends. I'm glad. Even though I'm afraid I am not one of them. His daddy is, though. They show the same two mothers live, talking, saying the same thing—keeping the heat on, keeping faith alive. And then the TV people show pictures of the dead women, all six and the seventh still not found, spread out at once, like a hand in poker. Or is that only five cards?

Looking in this bureau drawer and that bureau drawer for a misplaced pair of her mother's scissors, Carol heard Glenda's eldest daughter Paulette crying on TV, saying her mother had been through several ordeals in recent years, including breast cancer, and that she had "overcome it." She suddenly realized she had her new pair of scissors in her hand, but she wanted to use her mother's, why she couldn't really say.

"Mother, come look. It's the Thousand Islands."

Expecting another police report, Carol rushed into Melissa's room.

Gliding helicopter view of a multitude of islands, Discovery Channel.

"Well, I'll be . . ."

"Visitors to the Ten Thousand Islands of the Florida Everglades—"

"Oh. Not us."

"—will find every convenience before and after venturing into their midst by airboat."

"Imagine that."

The doctor had detected a spot on the x-ray. "Could be only a shadow maybe, but even so." So she cut into me, looking for "a shadow of interest." You, though, as usual, are safe. Safe until he discovers—if you cannot avoid exposure—that you have only one breast. They found "a foreign body," as they say, in you, too.

Above my hospital bed was a TV, but it was only a mirror, because I wanted to be free of their pictures for a while—the six victims. The seventh likely victim was not yet missing.

Lying in the very room where my mother used to nurse people well, or unto death, watching the nurses come and go, I wished I had finished nursing school and wondered why I didn't stick it out, and then again, I was glad I didn't. I would have been a nurse taking time off to be nursed. I saw the monotonous routine, but everything they do, *everything* they do, has a purpose. Like your whole life, Glenda. Even right this minute. Your purpose is to escape, escape.

The task force urged members of the killer's family to report any strange changes in routine, or if a man in any family keeps criticizing the police's methods, as if he knew what they did not. F does not do that, because you and he do not see the TV or turn on the radio. He has a cell, but he never turns it on. Nowhere to recharge it, anyway. Is he missed? Will his wife or boss or mother report *him* as a missing person?

I must come out of it now. I get like in a trance, a trance. Someone is coming. Someone? Why did I say that? I know who it is. It's my husband. It's him.

Her back to him, she pictured him—with one smooth flourish, he snapped open the refrigerator, jerked out a clinking bottle of beer, let the door swing

shut, a thudding suction sound, as if he had an audience. But not really showing off, to her or ever to anybody. Especially in public. A shy man in public,
even in church.

"Don't wander off. Supper will be on the table in about two shakes. Tim,
come help your mother and your sister put it on the table. Your father just
came in."

"I get so sick of the same old TV." Tim picked up the bowl of "smashed
potatoes," as his father called them, for him to repeat.

"*I* don't." Melissa carried the butter dish in both hands, as a butler would,
into the dining room.

"Tim, call your father to the table."

"Dad, Mom told me to tell you to come to the table."

Jack walked into the dining room, head far back, bottle straight up, drain-
ing the last of his beer.

She's safe. She's safe. She's safe.

Carol watched her husband and her eleven-year-old and her six-year-old
eat. Silently. My family, Glenda.

No, yours. I must concentrate on you and *your* family—Denton, Paulette,
Kendall, and Lydia, see *them* sitting down to supper, or do *you* call it "dinner"?

Holy Spirit, help me focus on Glenda.

Even when I am not consciously thinking out loud in my mind about you,
Glenda, I feel your presence, unbroken.

I wish I could see the International Bridge from one of my west windows.
Bridges lift my spirits, and that one is lovely, pale green, with red and green
lights at night blinking. Were you thinking of crossing it, just before he pointed
the gun at you? I overheard somebody telling another person that they have
opened the restored Mostar Bridge. Bombed during the Balkan wars, down
after a thousand years, and now back up. A very short, but very beautiful,
bridge between one country and another. I remember seeing before and after
pictures, and now it is restored to what it was before. I can see it as if I were
about to step onto it myself—into another country.

Glenda, I know you must've come to the Thousand Islands before, and I
know you must know how beautiful this region is. So my mother gave birth to
me in this house, this village, and so I live in one of the most beautiful places
in the world, another vast nation within sight northward, a great river flowing
past, islands of every shape and personality, east and west, almost two islands

for each inhabitant of our streets, daily immersed in sights that could stop your heart longer than a sneeze, and yet, look at him, Mister Jack Seabold, the master of my mother's house, oblivious. A fisherman like his grandfather and his ancestors until recently, and then a carpenter building boats, and now lays marble countertops throughout the area by day, lies on the living room couch by evening, too tired to break out of his genuine, first-attraction shyness.

And over here sits me, attuned to every sound of water and every break of icicle and cry of hawk and eagle and every bark of dog or doglike creature, and neither of us blissful. Rich folks come and go, even if their island houses stay, and put the profits of their lives into these castles and grand houses, cottages they call them, and Jack and I get this paradise for free, comparatively. Are they happier than we are? The happy-go-lucky tourists look the happiest, envious, too—of us. What about *that*? If beauty is truth, we're drowning in it. Is that all ye need to know? I took English, too, Paulette.

What I'm saying to you now, Glenda, I've said before, to Jack, and got a grunt, and have debated trying it out on Father. In the next life, maybe.

The silence at the table seemed a rude interruption.

You and F are talking. Keep talking.

"Mother, this tuna casserole is luscious."

"Thank you, Melissa."

Keep talking, Glenda. I'm listening.

"I agree with my grandfather." Jack cast a look around the table. "Do not thank your mother, who only cooked the food you eat, good or bad, but your Father in heaven who provided it."

Sounds familiar as a cough in the night.

"I never knew my great-grandfather." Tim looked down at his plate, well aware that he and his father had been over this before.

Glenda, I am an excellent cook, as the actual look on my husband's face, contrary to the words out of his mouth, proves. I got a lot of practice by having hot food on the table when my hardworking mother and my professing father came through that door, sometimes even at the same time, together, when my mother wasn't on duty as head night nurse.

* * *

45

Thank you, God, that he didn't take *me*.

I was there alone with him, Glenda, before you appeared out of nowhere, and F did not take me. Maybe because Melissa was with me, a saving grace.

But no, it was me he did not want. I do not look the look he seeks. On a grading scale of A to F, F gave me an F.

F is keeping you cuffed at night, and you two are still driving—even *you* are driving, looking for a safe place to pass the night.

The family unit—minus Tim for the moment—is parked in front of the TV, waiting for the news.

Jack is a Hunting Channel freak, but only to ridicule the hunters. Checks in often to the Weather Channel about water conditions for boating, no longer in the boat-building business. Never believes a word they say.

Tim's favorite show is *Without a Trace:* That's Tuesdays now.

In her own little room, on her own little battery-run TV set, Melissa watches Discovery, all the *C.S.I.*s, and reruns of *Friends* and of *Seinfeld.* "I am their most fateful fan." Melissa's voice is deep like Katharine Hepburn's, but she can do all the voices. That girl in *Seinfeld:* "The dingo ate yore ba-by." And everybody in *Everybody Loves Raymond:* Frank with his "Holy crap," and Deborah with her word for Raymond, "Idiot." "I like it when they yell at each other."

I have no TV favorites. I'm a nervous surfer. I hold the zapper. I automatically tune in to everybody else's favorite shows, and call to them when they wander.

"Channel Two's Deborah Swenson is live with Glenda Hamilton's three daughters, Paulette, Lydia, and Kendall.

"Paulette is an English teacher, Kendall is a pediatrician, and Lydia is a student at Jefferson Community College here in Watertown and plans to go into mass communications after graduation."

Lydia will one day report on achieving women and missing women on TV or in the papers.

I am learning tonight that Paulette's second husband is a contractor.

That Kendall's first husband was a high-school biology teacher.

I keep learning more and more about you—from the news and from overhearing people talk. The paper said Paulette is thirty-five—my age—so you must have been married before. Did you divorce him or did he divorce you or did he die? Is death itself like a divorce?

All three are very beautiful, Glenda, although Lydia is seriously overweight, as you know.

My husband, of course, said to your daughters on the TV, "You all look too old to be living with your mother."

I told him, "They don't. They just gathered in her living room for the TV."

"How do *you* know?"

He always uses that tone of voice that says, You who know nothing.

Maybe I know nothing about sports, but I read almost everything that's not on the sports page. I might even qualify as an expert on Iraq and the Sudan. Besides, the TV itself said, "We are in Glenda Hamilton's living room." Jack's problem is that he doesn't listen. To him, the problem is *everything*.

Paulette is on TV crying and saying again that you were on your way to visit your husband Denton in that high-class cancer hospital in New York City. A long drive. Let's listen to Paulette. "Our mother has never minded the three-hundred-sixty-mile, six-hour drive to Manhattan to visit our father in the hospital. We pray that her mysterious disappearance will have a happy ending."

The three of them on the wide, plush couch, Lydia mute the whole time.

Cut to Kendall's face now. "I am going to be with my father while my two sisters will remain here until my mother is found. She is very strong and resourceful. She will give a very logical explanation, laughing all the while. Just you wait."

Then Paulette's face again. "That's the way she is. Anybody can tell you that."

"Yeah, right." Jack cocked back in his recliner, crossing his soiled-white-socked feet, as if to prove himself right. "Dead as a doorknob is what she is." Carol stared at his engineer boots, parked by his chair. "Definitely not laughing."

Melissa panned the room with her broken kaleidoscope, the soiled Band-Aid still around her thumb.

I can trust Melissa to keep quiet about our late-night road excursions. She could keep a secret even under torture.

I slipped and told my husband I saw you, but when he asked where, I got out of it by saying "in the art museum in Watertown one time." If I told him exactly where, he would demand to know what I was doing at Tibbetts Point Lighthouse, and I need to keep my "get-away" drives secret, just as I am talking to you in the secrecy of my head.

Tim walked into the room, chewing the last of the Krispy Kremes, wiping his fingers on his dirty shirttail but not his sugar-coated lips. "What happened?"

"The cops struck out again tonight. Let that be a lesson to you, Tim."

"Oh, Dad."

"Don't 'Oh, Dad' me. It's life, son. Ever see a cop when you need one?"

"Yeah, like when my toy cut my thumb." Melissa kept her eye at the kaleidoscope.

"Oh, Dad, why does everybody say that all the time? Don't you watch *Cops?*"

"Frank was home sick the other day, leaving us no cop at all, until nighttime, when we now have two cops riding around Alexandria Bay sightseeing. That's a job I would not turn down." Jack shoved himself out of his recliner. "I leave you all to your own devices."

He's going out again, God knows where, and only God cares.

You are in my mind every minute of the day and into the night, and when I wake before it is light, I see your face, ever since your three daughters showed your face and I first watched that film clip of you on the evening news. And I hope and pray that keeping you fixed in my mind will help you keep yourself alive.

F wants attention, especially from women, especially from a woman like you, and you hope you are his first woman like you. He seems continually amazed that you two are together as you are, talking, riding back roads slowly, zigzagging down toward Manhattan. He keeps backtracking different rural routes, to evade police, so you are only so far as the tiny village of Rossie. And that's because he is afraid of exposing himself to police pursuit and capture.

By now, maybe F feels comfortable enough with you to stay in a motel.

I am still with you when I am not seeing you now, hearing you, touching you, smelling you. Words are things, are actions, my father would tell you. Yes. Refuse, Glenda, to be of a doubtful mind, because you and I are of one mind, striving together in the mind of the Spirit.

My husband just drove up.

"I need it for my work." In his arms was a box.

What he took out of the box was a computer.

He took over the walk-in closet he had built in their bedroom, converted it into a little office in no time.

But why? You're a countertop installer.

Jack went "out" again.

Carol grabbed her passport, always at hand, and Melissa's hand and took a drive over the International Bridge into Canada, trying to see at least the silhouette of the Sky Deck by moonlight.

I wish I didn't even have to take my six-year-old with me. But I do. My eleven-year-old is old enough to be alone in the house, but he is not responsible enough to baby-sit her yet. And his attitude. It is not every night, of course, only when my husband goes out himself somewhere for something. Then I jump in the car with my six-year-old and go.

Carol turned east toward Rockport, passing its little wooden Methodist church as she drove in, slowly cruising the village.

When she returned, she tucked Melissa into bed, her toy at her side. Are your dreams kaleidoscopic?

She opened her purse. Where did *that* come from? Windshield ice scraper, tiny pearls of thawed ice still in its webbed teeth.

A light showed through the fixed slats in the foldout closet doors.

He'd beaten her home.

She went into the living room and defied the TV with *Time* until the eleven o'clock news came on. But it was a repeat. Except that the policewoman said, "Why she ended up at the lighthouse, thirty miles north, and out of her way to New York, is a mystery."

"When did you come in?"

"A few minutes ago."

That Jack did not ask Carol where she and Melissa had been surprised her.

Some people suspect, I bet, I married him because I was pregnant.

People have always suspected—some are convinced—I had to marry Gordon because I was pregnant. But I was a virgin when he married me, and we never had a baby. No, I forgot, I did it with Bill that one time before he had to go to Desert Storm.

Maybe I just had the look of a girl who would get herself into trouble. Maybe the way I dressed. Maybe I looked easy. But I don't really know what that look is. And I have always been shy. Some shy people, I have noticed, are mean-talking. Oh, they're just covering up their deeper sensitivity, they say. Am I mean-talking? I don't think so. I must pay attention to myself and see if I am. Who would I talk mean *to*? That's a good question. To my six-year-old? I hope not. To my eleven-year-old? Well, there are problems with him sometimes. Is it me? Maybe. Why not say his father has a hand in his son's problems? Let *him* take some of the blame.

But nobody in this family talks very much to each other. Same on both sides. His mother and father seldom come over, but when they do, they just sit and not talk. That's fine with me. What would I say to them? His mother is a professional housewife, as opposed to amateur housewife, like me. Yet she never says a word. Leaves the comparison up to me. I get it. His father sold insurance until recently, won the regional award each year for the most sales. He could sell it to everybody except his son. A waste of money. Jack seems to enjoy getting a rise out of his father just to annoy me, so that his father will then launch into the same long, open-brochure spiel to us every time. What will I do if one of Jack's parents dies and he takes the other one into this house and I am alone with him or her all day long?

I'd rather it be Carl in this house. I really do love listening to Carl talk, tell stories about Korea, and how it would have been if Bill had come back from Desert Storm, married me, and gone to law school, me working to help him get through it.

Same with my father. He comes by, sits a while. Then goes. Now and then I run into somebody who had him in psychology classes at Jefferson Community College (maybe you did, too, Glenda, no, it was probably Radcliffe for you), and they rave about what a great teacher he is and how witty and how he's always eager to hang out with his students and his colleagues in the Student Union or Shorty's. He was never like that at home, among us. My grandfather always said my father was a loner. He does seem lonely. But when he is in front of a class or a convention audience or a motivational session for some big corporation, he doesn't speak or walk like a lonesome man. He's broken up into parts. But very likely he knows that. I am of two minds, he says, usually twice.

Melissa's imitation of his voice is uncanny. Melissa's not happy, maybe, but not unhappy. Even keel. Witty, for sure.

Yes, Tim's moody. But not *too*. Off and on, he wants to be an astronaut. So you can look down on your mother? I overheard my father say that to him, and Tim groaned. My father says Tim is like Jack, but he doesn't say Melissa is like me. I don't see Jack in Tim, but maybe he shows a side of Jack that Jack doesn't. I think Melissa is like my mother, not me. But if I am like my mother, as my father used to say, then Melissa *is* like me.

I like knowing such things. The only trouble in that is, how can you ever be sure? None of *your* daughters look like or act like *you*. I haven't seen a picture of your husband or your first husband. I only skim the society pages. How would

I know what I was looking at if I didn't see myself among you once in a while. 'The woman going on middle age who cruises the streets of this city in the old Oldsmobile held a gathering of all the folks she spies upon: her first husband Gordon, her old lover James and his family, her father, and sundry others.' For human interest, that beats the garden club. My father made the society page one time in a group shot. He sloughed it off. I majored in psychology at Syracuse, but when Bill died of that rusty nail infection during Desert Storm, I dropped out after only one year.

My mother was head nurse at Good Samaritan. Totally professional, totally reliable, totally without mystery, totally suicidal—all her life probably, without knowing it the whole time. Maybe I wouldn't be how I am if my father and my mother had talked more to each other and then to me and to my brother and we all sat around talking and laughing when I was growing up. Maybe the real stumbling blocks are excuses like that. After my mother shot herself, I rushed into the nursing program but dropped out when Jack kept saying, How can you see the house my mother keeps and let ours go like this? Like what? I asked, even though his answer is always the same. Like a ghetto.

I didn't mean to get off on myself like that. My point is that, even so, I wouldn't have been able to pull off what you have been pulling off. Talking to the Daylight Serial Killer, aka F, step by step, until you two are driving three hundred and some miles together to withdraw all your secret deposits from a little bank on Staten Island. That gives you a good stretch of time to find a way to break away from him.

But even if you make it to the bank and take out the money, the relationship you will have forged will protect you from any rash action. Because you know it's not the money he wants, even though he's probably a laborer of some kind who moves from job to job. It's what you have given him, being with a stranger in a way he's never had before. Two people talking. He thinks women mistreat him, and so he kills them in a rage. That's what my father teaches in his Intro to Abnormal Psychology classes, I suppose, but the profilers have said it all along. I learn a lot from listening to them and to the other experts who keep speaking on the television and talk radio shows. I might have made a good profiler myself. TV is all I get to see because my husband has gotten in the habit of taking the paper to his work site to read during his breaks and lunch, and he never brings it back. I never ask. I don't know where he went this morning. Maybe to see Thyre Mann, make plans for the search. He was gone when I got up. He does that sometimes. I'm glad. I can talk to you without fear of getting caught.

I will be talking to Melissa, my constant companion, or Jack, or Tim, or even Father, and I feel as though I am simultaneously talking to you. But it works the other way around, too. Sometimes when I talk to you or about you, one of them stands in the shadows, listening, as if spoken to.

Where are you going, Glenda?

I'm afraid to go to sleep, because F has turned off Highway 12 onto Highway 6, one of those back-back roads, with signs like ROUGH ROAD, NEXT 5 MILES, BLIND INTERSECTION, and DEAF PERSON AREA, I remember, long stretches, long stretches where the annual thaws have broken up the pavement, and then stretches of winding gravel road, winding and winding, those huge rocks scattered all around the landscape. I'm sorry, I'm sorry, I'm sorry. I've tried and I've tried, Glenda, but I just can't go with you into that forsaken region, huge boulders and ravines, and briars, right and left.

3

Jack spewed a mouthful back into his cup.

"It's a new brand. Give it a chance, why don't you?"

"My whole family, my whole life, nothing, nothing but Maxwell House coffee."

Melissa chirped, "Good to the last drop."

"Get that little brat out of here."

Melissa giggled.

The toast came out with more faces than usual. Melissa described each one. Tim rolled his eyes.

This morning the toast faces made Carol uneasy.

"I'm going to become a forensic anthropologist" was her way of expressing a forlorn wish, knowing Jack and Tim would give her those looks, but that Melissa would look up at the ceiling and nod in the affirmative. And they did.

He might still slit your throat with that knife. Shoot you with that pistol. Even though he seems calm and at ease with you and even charming, because the profilers say he is good at that, putting women at ease, especially self-possessed women like you and the others, so he can strike. He doesn't just jump you out of nowhere the way most rapist-killers do, even though he broke his MO with you. So we—*you* need to watch for a chance to escape, now that you have won his confidence. You didn't ask in terror the way the others probably did, Where are you taking me? Even my husband hates hearing that question. He will say to us, "Get in the car." And I gather my brood and we go get in the car, like he says. He never goes and gets in the car and sits there waiting for us to come or blow his horn in a sudden rage. If we don't hop to it, he says, "If you people are not in that car in two minutes, I am leaving you to your own devices." That is usually okay with us, but then again, if he takes off and leaves us behind, we have to worry about how he's going to behave when he gets back, reeling back up the sidewalk, sullen. So to keep him on an even keel, we make it to the car before the deadline, and wait for him to come to us. And we know better than to ask, "Where are you taking us?" All he does is take us to Clayton so his mother can see her grandchildren, give them stale cookies, or something routine like that. No nice surprises, no special places. Well, the movie in Watertown once in a blue moon, or a hamburger and a shake, if he doesn't like what I am in the middle of cooking. Sometimes I don't care for it myself.

It's not only that I am afraid for you—no, I'm not afraid for you, I'm not forgetting *who* you are. I don't mean socially and because of your husband being who and what *he* is, a prominent doctor. That probably—well, certainly—does work into who you are. I mean the who that was there from childhood, vivaciously self-reliant from the word *go*. Admired by children who were like me. A role model for us. Going into the stone house that first night north of Chippewa, captive to public enemy number one. Not that you aren't afraid, you're human, but you have faith. "In this world ye shall have tribulations. But be of good cheer. I have overcome the world." Of good cheer. That's you, no matter what the circumstances. Even if it's sometimes an act you put on, it's a hit. It's the kind of thing you can maybe say at the right moment—to F. I'm no Bible-verses-memorizing vacation-Bible-school graduate, I just happened onto that verse and it never faded, partly because it's a little mysterious. *How* did Jesus "overcome" the world in a way that made Him think to tell us to be of good cheer? You have tried everything and will keep trying, and religion is one way to keep F on an even keel—the straight and narrow, as the Good Book says. No matter how evil . . . But what is evil? and what is just downright mean? and when and where do they step over the line?

In the morning time, I have only about thirty minutes to talk to you, before I have to go up and wake them all up to another day. Somehow talking to you makes me want to read my old diary that I kept from when I was only a few years older than Melissa, up until James—the love of my life—told me he was committing himself to his pregnant wife. And then I hid it where nobody would think to look or come across it accidentally. Down here in the basement behind these quarts of peaches and apples and pears my mother preserved the summer she died—well, shot herself. I don't call that dying. I call that shooting yourself, deliberately. When she had a perfect marriage, a perfect profession, a perfect son—or so everyone always said or thought—and a near-perfect daughter.

This house is mother's, she willed it to me, and my husband loves it because each month rent or mortgage does not take a huge chunk out of his paycheck and he gets to lord it over his buddies, bowling in Watertown or at the games—so many games, one season ends as another begins, overlaps, actually—or at the watering hole, as he calls that beer joint. Beer Bead Pub. This is a drinking town, he says, and takes another drink. He's not loud about it, he's the silent type, rock bottom, he's shy, which can get on your nerves, too. You know, Carol, Jack is very shy. His mother promoted him to me, his having that nice quality. "But only in front of people," she said.

Jack says I get on his nerves when I talk a blue streak, which is seldom, and then when I'm quiet for long stretches, he says, "You get on my nerves, creeping around. Laugh. Cry. Shout or something. You're just like my mother, with that look in her eyes," he says, "like she's looking out to sea for her ship to come in." Yeah, she does say that quite often.

With no place to stay, you were forced to pull over onto a deserted road and into dark woods and sleep in the truck, you handcuffed to that eyebolt in the floorboard, he hunched behind the steering wheel, tall, one leg sticking straight out, the other cocked up, almost touching your shoulder.

What would Jack say if he knew I am talking to *you?* Nonstop. I don't really know. That's just it. I don't really know. Even though basically, he is predictable. I know exactly why I am talking to you, and that's unusual for me—to know exactly. He still doesn't know I saw you at the actual scene. He would accuse me of taking his six-year-old daughter where serial killers prowl. Even the simple reason why I was at the lighthouse there would freak him out. Or did I have a not-so-simple reason, something to do with my next surgery appointment—on the cutting edge. That I need to do something on my own when he's playing poker, bowling, or whatever, even if it's only short drives, daylight or into the night on the highways out of this town or over the International Bridge into Canada, into Ivy Lea or Rockport, Kingston, even as far as Gananoque—"place on the rocks by swift-moving water," the Indian meaning. That's not enough for anybody, of course, but that's something. Well, whose fault is it but my own? I must quit talking about myself and talk exclusively to you. Are you listening?

I said "serial killer," but they haven't linked your abductor to the Daylight Serial Killer yet, because they say your body has not been found—and they never will. They come up every day or so with a person of interest, as you know from all these months since the first body—Theresa Finley—was found, with a person of interest. They show a sketch of somebody I hope never walked this earth, he is so weird, like a man from Mars, with what looks like a stuck-on nose. And they show a photo of the type of van, at first, and now the pickup truck one or two witnesses—anonymous me, for one—say they saw drive away from the scene or that was seen cruising the neighborhood in Watertown where six of the women lived.

Now we are both on the move together with a "person of interest." The three of us.

You may at any moment lose your life, and so, lose everything that is yours in this world. If you were to take an inventory of what you truly own, what would you list? Not just people and things—that's easy—but try including feelings, thoughts, imaginings. Well, take people, too. How do you "own" children, even though they came out of your own body? Take things, too. In three hundred words or less for a value of 20 percent on the final, Carol, How and what in sense do you own the things you own? Next question: What would you *rather* own, and why? Sounds like you know who. What must I do to be alive an hour from now? That is the question. Forgive me, Glenda. You do not have time to answer such questions.

After Jack, followed by Tim, cleared out, Carol went into the living room to be with Melissa.

Melissa looked up from a brown study. "I bet you were just like me when you were my age."

Carol was delighted. "I wouldn't put it past me."

She lay down on the living room rug and looked up into Melissa's face. "What do you want to do today, kid?"

"Go to that old deserted drive-in movie place again."

"I see they put up a no-trespassing sign. And it's too cold."

"I know."

* * *

"I need to take your history, Mrs. Seabold."

Do *I* need to take my history? Maybe *I* need to take my history.

"As a matter of fact," my Father would say, "what the hell is it?"

Turned out, what the nurse meant was syphilis and bowel movements and fluctuations in weights and all. "No, no, no, no," I said.

So I too have been tested. I finally got a mammogram, here in Alexandria Bay. Then Monday of last week, I underwent the operation in Watertown at Good Samaritan Hospital, where my mother nursed for many years, even before I was born, and where your husband doctored, maybe even with my mother assisting him.

Dr. Christina Trenton told me later that morning that she found "a silent killer," but that it's an early detection, that radiation may shrink it. They keep you no longer than they have to, but in my case, Dr. Trenton had nicked an artery—"it never happens, unless it does"—and she kept me a few more days for observation.

They sent me home. To the house. I am here. This house. Still here. There is the couch. There's the TV set. Everything still here, whether I died or lived. There is that old, old picture on the wall of Boldt Castle on Heart Island that I could not remember when I lay on my back confined to that hospital bed. I have the same view now—the real thing—through our picture window. Routine. The same routine. As if nothing had happened. If I had died and been resurrected, would they treat me any different? Even you, by now, have, with F, a routine. A very precise routine already, but you have to adapt it to different places. On the run. Evasive tactics.

You two still have plenty of money to keep on the go because his own money has not run out and then there are your more than adequate funds for that visit to your husband in the hospital in Manhattan.

Free of the cancer, I feel no different—like when I lost my virginity—but I know I am. When you are free of F, you will never be the same, will you? You and not you. They leave their mark. Oh, don't get me wrong. I am not what you call unhappily married, if you compare me with what I see and hear all around me every day, around the village and out in the world, Iran, Iraq. Women and their husbands under the Taliban—way under. The Sudan. Female circumcision in Africa.

Look at Afghanistan, imagine the world, all around the world, the abductions and rapes and murder of women every minute of every day. When I was nine or so, I had imagined such dangers and trembled, but looked at my father, my grandfather, all the men around me, young and old, and relaxed, thinking they were doing something about it, that in time they would change the world. Just for me.

And right here in my little neighborhood. People don't let other people see much, but you see little things, little things, and they mount up, until you just know.

Was *that* there before? A man's belt, buckle shape of a horse on the bare floor.

Carol had to get out. She sat in the Oldsmobile. Turning the ignition key filled the car with mournful singing.

> It was early one morning in the month of May
> Oh the wind and the rain
> Two lovers went walking on a hot summer's day
> A crying the dreadful wind and rain

Carol imagined it must be NPR.

> Then he knocked her down and he kicked her around
> Oh the wind and the rain
> Then he knocked her down and he kicked her around
> A crying the dreadful wind and rain

If I were in the mood, I could never find a song like this.

> He hit her in the head with a battering ram
> Oh the wind and the rain
> He hit her in the head with a battering ram
> A crying the dreadful wind and rain

I can't stop now.

He threw her in the river to drown
Oh the wind and the rain
He threw her in the river to drown
A crying the dreadful wind and rain

She never listened to the radio. Tim must have gotten the keys off the kitchen ring and gone out to play like he was driving—to music, anything, and liked NPR from Watertown, of all things.

Where's Melissa?

"Watching TV, I see."

"*Discovery.*" Melissa did not look at Carol.

"Discover this, why don't you? When Carol Helvy was six years old, fact—"

"Going on seven?"

"When Carol Helvy was six years old, whatever, fact number one—there were only two channels in the Thousand Islands, usually out of focus or snowed in, like Tug Bluff Plateau in a snowstorm; fact number two, no personal computers, no information superhighway; fact number three, no cell phones, no voice message gizmos, fact number four—"

"Why are you telling me all this while my *Discovery* is on?"

Is it your testimony here today that when asked why you were reeling off facts about life as it once was, your reply was a perplexed silence?

I don't know what came over me.

Driving aimlessly around Alexandria Bay, she kept her eye out for the coyote, everywhere she went.

"Do you have the bones back there with you, Melissa?"

"Safe and sound."

To lure the coyote out into the open, hoping she could slowly entice it to eat out of her hand, so she could tell her father, or Tim, or Jack—Frank was suddenly in her rearview mirror in his patrol car right behind her—or Frank.

Noticing she was on Fuller, she drove past Bach's Inn, then River Hospital, seeing herself getting a mammogram there a month or so ago, past the Episcopal church at the base of a bluff—aware that she was anchoring herself in the moment—to Scenic View Park so Melissa could walk across the bridge over to the tiny island, but a chain kept them off.

Frank's behind me again. He's suspicious of me, or he just likes me, or both, or neither.

Driving impulsively on toward Watertown, she left Frank behind.

To the left, a few acres of blighted trees, and then just up ahead, right off the highway, those three huge ravens, statues, Adirondack Mountains running alongside in the distance. ROAD WORK.

I am trying to see Watertown through *your* eyes, Glenda. There comes up the Old Jail Antiques place. Do you frequent that place? And we have that new beauty parlor in our old jail. Silly, I know, but I feel a link with you. I'm pulling over to go in there.

Snow distorts the public statues on three islands in the Public Square, the Soldiers and Sailors Monument, Governor Roswell F. Flower, if you count the bandstand.

Oh, yes, Father, you used to drive me around them to show me.

On Clinton Street, the very fine homes, but Paddock Street is almost as good as the best. I think of this as your town, "Garland City" when they used to put bunting on all the windows and all the statues in the square, but you and I lived here at the same time back when I was married to Gordon and in love with James. Monumental old buildings, not just the library and its dome, but the post office, the courthouse, and these churches—Catholic, Episcopal, Baptist—are so huge. Which is yours, Glenda?

Carol tried to identify Glenda's house just by intuition, but failed. She felt guilty consulting the address 411 gave her.

Odd name, isn't it, Watertown? The great water power. That great fire way back let the town show off that power.

"I don't remember any of these streets, Mother."

"That's because we're strangers here."

"Let's go somewhere else."

There's your front door.

Take a good look at your front door, Glenda. One day soon, maybe even this evening, you will walk through that door again on fashionable Paddock Street. If I were to walk up on the porch and ring the bell, one of your daughters would come to the door, hoping it is you and not the police, or the police bringing you home, not the police bringing your children the final news. Whether it is you or the police, the television cameras will be there in a flash.

Your smile will be live for the cameras, as it is now for F. Your smiling face, the face I see in each picture they show on Jack's huge TV screen.

And maybe F will be in the picture, too. Shuffling, ankles linked by a short chain, hands cuffed in front of his orange suit. I've seen that before. We have all seen it before. In this town, and in every other. Sometimes they smile for the cameras, like gentlemen. Sometimes they hide their faces. Sometimes they walk like they are in somebody else's nightmare.

I am glad I have your front door in my eye bank. Whatever good I am doing you will help to bring you to that door. I wish I could be there to watch you step gracefully over the threshold. A sight to see. A sight for my sore eyes. I did not sleep well.

Before F erupted into your life, did I see you in the flesh, here in Watertown, unaware?

Have you already broken free, and have I passed by you today, unaware?

Aware that she had parked in front of Glenda's house—conspicuous—to be reported as "a person of interest," Carol very slowly drove away, down the street, as an innocent person might.

As she passed, she glanced at all the doors.

What is that wreath doing on that door?

"I going to sicken and die."

"Melissa, where in the world did you hear that one?"

"I don't know, but it fits how I feel."

* * *

What am I doing here, Glenda? If I can see your daughter, listen to her talk, shake her hand. . . . Melissa says she's feeling much better, and I know it's not because she is afraid of doctors, especially women doctors. She is always full of questions and sometimes even ventures her own answers in advance.

Look at her.

Anybody in this room, any mother, would probably say she certainly doesn't look sick.

So your daughter will certainly catch on to that.

"Are you sure you don't hurt?"

"Mother, I told you."

"Okay, then."

Maybe I should be asking myself that question. Carol, do you hurt? If so, where and how bad is it?

Am I here as an excuse just to meet Kendall, a way of getting close to you, Glenda? I'm suspicious of my motive now.

"Please forgive us. We are feeling better now. Sorry."

"That's all right. Dr. Hamilton is behind schedule anyway. She just got back from New York City—an illness in the family, you know."

"Yes. Of course. Thank you. Have a nice day."

Were you ever divorced? Oh, yes. I remember. But there's so much I don't know about you. But then, too, does anyone know everything about you? They raised the question, What was Glenda Hamilton doing at Tibbetts Point Lighthouse, the opposite direction, and a bizarre difference, from the destination she gave her daughters, although your daughters haven't raised the question themselves on TV.

In Flower Public Library, Carol was aware that the Flower family funded most of the high-style structures in Watertown. I am looking you up, under the great dome of the Roswell P. Flower Memorial Library on Washington, where your career has often taken you, I am sure. Cranking one of those what's-its. And discover that you turned up in Watertown from Barstow, New Mexico, where folks called you "Boots" Balbin, father from Argentina, mother from Athens, Ohio. That explains your dark looks and your demeanor, only verging on arrogance because of the southern tone. Me, I'm from the frozen north, but you don't have to tell me that that is no excuse for anything.

Says here on this screen your two oldest daughters are by your first husband who left you, married his young secretary, and practices law in Georgetown, D.C. Your second husband, Denton Hamilton, is a sixty-year-old surgeon, father of Lydia, your youngest, the one who goes to Jefferson Community College, overweight, I notice, and, for all I know, may be sitting in one of my father's classes at this very moment, worried more about you than passing my father's tests, and in the distant past, my mother may have worked with your husband at the Good Samaritan Hospital. Which raises questions neither you nor I care or dare to address. Denton's first wife, Emily, died in a boating accident in the Thousand Islands, and in your house also lives his youngest son by his first marriage, his oldest being now in Afghanistan with the Special Forces.

I do not like to dwell upon the women who were taken before you, but here's my chance—while Melissa is content to pull huge reference books off the shelves, open each of them once, ponder the left and right pages, then replace them as neatly as any librarian.

Looking at a map in the newspaper that showed each island in the Alexandria Bay region where the women had been found over the past six years gave Carol a sense of control and inspired her to consult the atlas and pinpoint all the Alexandrias and Thousand Islands on the two-page-spread world map. Seeing Venice, Italy, on the map, she took delight in noting that Alexandria Bay too consisted of an equal proportion of land and water, though not surrounded, not an island as Wellesley is, just across the river from Alexandria Bay. Closing the huge book shut it all up in her own mind, and she felt less confined. She shut her eyes and imagined lighthouses one by one illuminating all those places.

The women so far are all from Watertown, like you. Not forgetting that Watertown, too, was once my own town. Maybe F thinks the Thousand Islands is a kind of Eden that he won't let the evil in himself spoil, by killing us there, except that one Watertown girl he killed in Alexandria Bay.

I want to know more about each woman. But you come between. Even so, I know all that is public now, but also where each one worked and lived. Let the names be given, let us not forget. Look over my shoulder at

Theresa Finley, 29, marketing consultant.

Lorna Massey, 27, owner of a high-end dress shop.

Ashley Corbett, 23, personal secretary.

Courtney Fritz, 25, computer technician.

Kaleesha Washington, 29, nurse.

Danielle Santini, 32, yoga instructor.

Kathy Donovan, 35, advertising executive, her body unfound.

Carol memorized each name, a kind of memorial, and recited them as she and Melissa left the library and vowed to recite them often.

Caught up in a fit of compassion, wrenching her guts, she stopped the car so suddenly, it skidded on the ice, stopped against the icy snow piled up along the curb. She sprung out of the car, bent over, convulsed in dry heaves.

Behind the wheel again, she waited for the trembling to subside, silently, slowly reciting their names.

Christ's compassion, Reverend Fredrika Sensibar had preached, was not from the heart—an organ that feels nothing—but from the gut, from which our deepest feelings of love, anger, and nausea come.

Keeping up talking to you only makes for more wear and tear on my nerves because I don't just have my husband and my two kids and my mother—well, not her—to worry about now, but you, too, your not knowing what comes next. Not that F will hurt you badly, because I know, maybe more than you do, that you will overcome this crisis situation. I hope I'm helping, with my prayers and my constant thinking about you and talking to you. Let me do the worrying for you. You keep your mind on how to handle F.

What is this bridge doing here? I thought it was—used to be over there, didn't it? No. I'm *on* the damn thing.

"How 'bout we go visit Bill's daddy again?"

"How come you didn't marry Bill in the first place?"

"We weren't compatible, and Desert Storm swallowed him up."

"Oh. Yeah. You told me the first time."

Bill's father was asleep among the other old folks in wheelchairs. She woke him with a kiss.

"I don't want to be here, Carol."

"I know, Carl."

"Can't you do something?"

"I've tried. Remember?"

"How about your husband? I'll bet he has connections?"

"Jack? Lord, no, he's just a kitchen counter installer—and ex–boat carpenter, ex-fisherman."

"Oh. Yeah. I forgot. I was thinking of Gordon."

I do not like to think of my first husband, Glenda. No, sometimes, I do, compared with Jack, or— "Do they mistreat you here?"

"Oh, no. They are very nice. It's just the idea of being among all these old people."

"I wish I could take you home with me, Carl. I always love to hear you talk."

"Will you talk for *me?*" Melissa looked up from her slapdash mended kaleidoscope.

"Even if I was a real relative, these days a retired person like me is a burden. Now if Bill was alive . . ."

Melissa looked up into the kaleidoscope.

"I miss him, too."

Don't think I'm not with you, Glenda.

"Desert Storm! Desert Storm . . . and now Iraq."

"Yes."

When Carol and Bill went on daytime dates, they saw Carl, standing at the busiest intersections—where a traffic light was out, or breaking up congestion in the square—among the islands of statues and monuments, about to retire, but a commanding presence in the heart of Watertown, "a fixture," the feature story on him in the Watertown *Daily Times* called him on his retirement.

"This one time, Bill says, 'Feels funny on a date to have your own dad directing you to stop, go, turn left.' And I said I didn't mind, and he says, 'I didn't say I minded, did I?' I just said, 'It feels funny,' and I told him I could imagine. 'But by now, I feel like I know your dad.'"

"If he had come home, would you two . . . ?"

"I don't know. Probably. We didn't really break up."

"It's like Korea here. Hemmed in. Can't break out. And at night, the Chinks swarm over the snow."

"Don't say 'Chinks.'" Melissa pointed at Carl.

I'm here, Glenda.

"What did she say?"

"She's just talking. Time to pick up and go, Melissa."

"When you coming back to see me?"

"Soon. Real soon."

"Exactly when? So I can look forward to it. You're all I've got, Carol."

"Whenever I can get away."

"Don't let 'em hem you in. And don't be a stranger."

"What? Oh. No, I won't."

"And bring that wisecracking kid when you come."

"Sure. You'll come with me, won't you, Melissa?"

"If I can get away."

They laughed at her, and Melissa finally laughed with them.

"As you go out, Carol, do me a big favor, will you?"

"If I can."

"Take all these old people with you."

In the car, Carol knew Melissa would bring it up again. "Mother, tell me again who Carl and Bill are?"

"Bill Amber was almost your daddy, and Carl was almost your granddaddy."

Melissa giggled as Carol knew she would.

Remembering, Carol stood beside Bill at the open door of the military transport bus. Bill's eyes, looking at her, created a zone around her that excluded everybody and everything.

As Bill backed away from her, she turned to keep from seeing him turn his back toward her.

Then his face at the oily window of the bus brought the desert in Kuwait suddenly very near. His death by infection from stepping on a rusty nail before the invasion was vague.

But two years later, I married Gordon the ex-marine, the civil engineer, and we had our differences over my desire to go to work, and then it just happened with James, an office affair, and then, after Gordon divorced me, in good time, as they say, I met your father, Melissa, and he or James or maybe even Gordon that last time in the kitchen got me pregnant with your brother. But that's a long story that I may never tell *you,* but probably must one day tell Tim.

What would *you* have done, Glenda?

Carol drove away from the gracious old county building, which her mother told her once had an isolation wing for TB patients, making Carol at Melissa's age see it in the fog and snow as a giant, white-winged bird. The long, old county buildings, the old folks' home, the old TB wards, condemned to demolition soon, maybe the whole historic structure in time.

Coming out of the parking lot there onto Coffeen, she did a sharp impulse left onto the entrance road to Jefferson Community College, a short drive through "the forest primeval," her father called it, so thick a DEER CROSSING sign stood halfway in.

Carol hung around outside the lecture hall door.

There he goes, tossing that gallstone up and down, just waiting for someone in this new class to ask, "Pardon me for asking, Professor, but what is that thing you keep tossing up while you're waiting for one of us—"

"For *you,* sir."

"—to answer your questions?"

"That, sir, is my philosopher's stone. The rest is silence."

Yes, but why? Because Mother was your nurse when you got it removed (by Dr. Denton Hamilton, perchance?), and/ or because it's a ritual for dealing with the fear of death? Philosophically speaking?

Did Mother sit in this very lecture hall when she was here in training, and did she then reappear at your bedside as your nurse, and did you recognize her as your former student, just as she surely recognized you as her former professor?

A marriage made in heaven, someone at her mother's funeral had said.

Maybe it was, and maybe it wasn't. How can I help but wonder, Father, uninformed as I am?

While she watched, no student actually asked about the stone.

You would feel comfortable in the company of my father, Glenda, voted Jefferson Community College's most popular teacher last year for the fifth time in his career. Big fish in a little pond, he holds examples of fuzzy thinking up for mass ridicule.

"'Killing me won't bring anybody back to life.' The condemned man's last words a world away down in Texas last night answered a question we cannot imagine anybody having asked him. An answer he hoped, one supposes, would persuade them not to execute him. Then he adds insult to injury when he apologizes. 'But I'm sorry for any pain I may have caused anybody.' A mind that works that way could be at ease killing another human being."

Carol had a question for her favorite professor. Out in the hall, she almost raised her hand. What way did your wife's mind work? Once you have answered that one, would you answer this one, please, What way does your daughter's mind work?

Next question, Carol.

Glenda, was that you?

Carol and Melissa sat on a bench facing the huge clock, set in a tall, stand-alone pillar, watching the students mill around or rush straight to the next class.

Maybe it will do *you* good, Glenda, if I see Lydia in the flesh, not just on TV.

The TV informed me what Lydia's major is—Mass Comm. She may be sitting in seat number so-and-so right now, taking notes, even have a crush on my father.

That one looks like Lydia. No. I will know her when I see her.

Carol watched her father walk right on past her.

"Daddy!"

He did not stop.

"Father!"

He hesitated, slowed, turned.

"It's me."

"I can see that."

"You didn't recognize my voice?" Or me from the back?

"No one has ever called me 'Father,' much less 'Daddy' in the quad before. Hello, Melissa. Is your mommy taking you for a stroll in the groves of academe?"

Usually mute in her grandfather's presence, Melissa, away from him, imitated not only his phrasing but his very voice. Coming up behind Carol, she had startled her one morning. "I'm of two minds about that."

"It's like a park here. Nicer than our little park in Alexandria Bay."

"I'm late for my two o'clock."

He doesn't look like anybody's father, certainly no one's daddy. Should I remind him of who I am? Imagine, Daddy, that I'm the kid in seat number

203, who sometimes sits in 204 and throws off the roll. Remember the kid in the high chair who tosses her oatmeal to get you to take your nose out of that book, thick as the Bible?

"We'll see you then." Carol held her hand to her forehead, a sunshield that felt like a salute.

"I see you here at a distance sometimes. Wandering around like a lost soul."

"I am the Wandering WASP."

That was the best she could give him, but he seemed to like it, might even use it in class today, find a way to fit it into the flow.

"Take care."

"You, too."

Holding Melissa's hand, she watched her father's back until he turned into Jules Center.

Was it spite that kept me from telling him that I will step up to death's door again this coming Monday?

* * *

Carol was listening closely to the registrar until he stacked her application papers sharply on his desk. "You would have to start the nursing program all over again. For one thing, the program has changed, been updated, but even so, the rule is, you'd have to repeat. And then there's your personal history. You seemed to have dropped out for no valid reason. I need to have confidence that you . . ."

"What I lack in confidence, I seem to make up for in prevarication. But I assure you, sir, I do intend to reform myself."

God is in the details. No, Tim, I think it's Satan. Such as my sweat. Times and places and situations when it just happens and I know people know.

"Be that as it may, are you willing to repeat?"

"Sir, I want to be a nurse like my mother, who—"

"I knew your mother."

Did I? Did Father?

I'm not the only such.

"What?"

"Nothing, honey, mommy's just talking to herself."

68

"Yeah, and thinking. I wouldn't want to be a nurse."

I'm not sure I would either. The textbooks give me a headache and the teachers are irritable. Glenda would make a great nurse. Wouldn't you?

"Well, your grandmother May was a nurse."

"You told me."

* * *

Carol and Melissa fell in with the students who were drifting in late.

She raised her hand.

Did you register in this course?

At birth.

I see. He seemed to. And your question is . . . ?

Is Glenda Hamilton alive?

She is with her abductor. Somewhere.

Thank you, Professor Helvy.

You are quite welcome.

In the restroom, Glenda's youngest daughter, Lydia, stared at her private reflection—as a young woman too fat—in the public mirror, weeping. Then she shifted focus to Carol in the mirror. I want to find myself.

Because many others have abducted you.

* * *

The constant roar of Interstate Highway 81 running along the back of the campus disturbed the forest primeval.

The huge YOUR ONE-STOP CAREER CENTER sign on a red building she usually took as a deliberate reproach.

The Child Care Building folks won't let me leave Melissa there until I am a student again.

She forgot, then remembered that it was in the lot next to the John Foster Dulles Building that her car was parked, Father's hand-me-down Oldsmobile with the long-out-of-date faculty parking sticker.

"I saw what happened. Anybody can hit a deer, Mrs. Seabold, even on this campus. You needn't feel stupid, ma'am."

"She didn't say she felt stupid."

"Keep quiet, Melissa. The grown-ups are talking."

"Way the deer was running into the woods, you probably only clipped it, just barely, so. . . ."

"So, do you have to ticket me?"

"Unfortunately, yes. I'm very sorry. A rule I cannot break."

Having signed the form, she impulsively added her telephone number.

* * *

In Shorty's, a block above the college, just before the turn onto Interstate Highway 81 to the northeast, Carol and Melissa sat side by side, satisfying a voracious appetite for double cheeseburgers and French fries, virtuously turning down their favorite banana cream pie.

Below Jefferson Community College, at the bottom of a steep hill on Coffeen Street, named for the old, old father of the city, Carol passed the fairgrounds, where, when she was old enough, she went alone into the spook house because she didn't want her father to comment on everything, making it another experience with her father, rather than a pure scare-the-hell-out-of-you experience.

Given the fact that I loved James more than any man I have ever known, why doesn't that count in the eyes of the world as a marriage, over and above the first mistaken one to Gordon and this dull one to Jack? Maybe because to James, I was merely an office fuck. I'll bet *you* were never an office fuck. I ramble.

She was aware that now that she had Glenda to worry about and talk to, she did not feel the same urgent need to tour routinely the scenes of her misfired pursuits and her missed opportunities and her fantasy futures as a diversion from her present situations. James's wife in the flesh could ruin her whole day. Nothing must distract me from you, Glenda.

But she felt habit drawing her back. And Glenda was such a contrast, a vivid presence in her mind, almost as a third passenger in the car, sometimes beside her, sometimes in the back seat beside Melissa, that visits to Carl and drive-bys, such as James's house and their favorite restaurant, made her feel she was not neglecting Glenda.

James's secretary had hired her to answer the phone, file, and do errands, et cetera, so that when she first laid eyes on James himself, he walked into the outer office as her boss—every detail fine-tuned, but electric, his blue eyes sending the charge into every part of his body and what his body wore, and he had bossed her immediately, standing back far enough from the front of her desk to display all of himself, feet apart as in a stance, arms down, almost a foot out from his body, his fingers splayed, straight, but flickering, as if eager to get his hands on the first task on a long list of tasks, the first ten already keenly in mind.

I've never seen anybody walk into a room that way, she'd almost said aloud, but heard herself saying it loudly in her head.

He smiled as if he had heard, and said, "Take a joyride in my new car." He tossed the bright keys onto her desk. "And don't come back until you have a glittering smile on your face."

James loved to uproot people with such outlandish gifts, not of the things themselves, but of such actions as that.

"Go outside, Carol, and smell some flowers and do not come back until you do."

"Carol, don't just sit there. Jump up and run out and build us all a snow-man."

"You know, Carol, if you take off your dress, I promise not to give a damn."

He never gave me a damn thing, except electricity. And surprises, like calling from Venice or Costa Rica on days full of appointments in Watertown. "I forgot my toothbrush. Buy me one and bring it to me. Place Vendome, Ritz Hotel, Paris. You can't miss it."

James Marquart—Type A heart, overachiever, impulsive, total control, hard-focused confidence. Electric touch.

You and James were made for each other, Glenda.

That's him, walking out of our favorite restaurant. That's James. And that's not his wife with him.

Do you suppose he picks our favorite restaurant for the same reason I drive by it?

If he had kept his promise and divorced Joyce and married me eleven years ago, I would not be talking to you, Glenda. Or maybe I would. Maybe I would still be me, just as I am. Or if Gordon and I had tried harder to sort out our differences before I went to work for James and fell under his spell, a whole jury all in one.

Your breath stinks, you wish you could tell him. I don't see how you stand it. Not that F has forced a kiss on you. He doesn't have to do that, because sitting beside him, one hand cuffed, sometimes both, you get whiffs when he turns to talk.

And he talks more and more. You keep your hands where he is not so aware that he has you bound up, so he isn't always aware he's talking about himself to a captive. He never refers to himself as what he is, but stresses his respect for women that he learned from his momma. You try to match everything he says about himself and his life with something about your own life, but less, so that he's always the one in the spotlight, which is where he seems he always likes to be. Attention. He craves it, more now that he has it than when he merely craved it.

I don't have to tell you to listen carefully to every word he utters. Very carefully. Even the silences. Especially what he might have said but doesn't say outright. And the expressions on his face that go with every word, even in profile. I feel as if I have spent my life watching their mouths in profile. And when they turn full-face toward you, that's when you freeze and watch and listen most intensely. And their voices when their backs are turned or coming from another room, or coming up the stairs, even from behind closed bathroom doors at the top of the stairs, or from under the floor, coming up from the basement, or from outside when the motors stop. There's always a motor running somewhere, and then you can relax, as if they are snoring. It stops, and then it's like they are suddenly awake and will probably yell to you or scream for you. To answer the door, the phone, or bring toilet paper to the bathroom.

"Why do we go to the same places allatime?"

I like to keep in touch. "Just because."

"There must be a reason."

"When do you need to know?"

Melissa giggled. "If you told me, you'd have to kill me."

Carol's voice pulling one-liners out of their repertoire, and Melissa's response was as stimulating as her finger tickling Melissa.

When the front door opened, Carol sped away from in front of James Marquart's house.

I look for them everywhere I go, hoping, fearing I will see Joyce, her, at least, with their twins, maybe.

She took Melissa to Thompson Park on the hillside at the end of town opposite from the college where her father would be teaching now. "Designed by Olmsted, as was Central Park and the Biltmore," her father often said, delighted to instruct. "And the hills around are like Rome, the Black River bisecting, as the Tiber bisects Rome," her father said, sneering at the contrast.

As Melissa watched the kids sledding down hill toward the circle, Carol slipped out of the car.

"I thought you quit!" Melissa's hands were cupped around her mouth to create a megaphone to enhance the declarative tone of her comment through the closed car window.

Carol imitated her, a cigarette held out elegantly, bending forward at the waist, wishing she had put her coat on before getting out of the car. "I did! I did! I have quit often in my long life! Ergo, I can quit anytime I put my mind to it!"

Melissa rolled down her window. "And you, my friend, are out of your mind."

"Stop doing that red head guy from TV around me."

They watched the kids sledding.

"Lock your door." The first body—Theresa Finley, may God rest your soul—was found here before you were born, Melissa, honey.

Glenda, you and I have been many times to Thompson Park Zoo and Snow Slide, and the park circle for skating, on our own or with our husbands, lovers, children.

And will come again. Perhaps together.

But does that mean F might come here again?

And there they come, for God's sake, Joyce and her three-year-old twins, Brent and Peter, into the park, as if on time for an appointment. Tim, but if you were here now, big brother, you could see your twin blood brothers. *If* they are. The boy with three fathers? Gordon, James, Jack—mingled semen?

The child Joyce was pregnant with at the same time I was pregnant with Tim—both are in school right now, different towns. James is certain he's the father of Joyce's eleven-year-old, Skylar, but my Tim could be his, too, or not.

She is not beautiful in face or figure. But the sound of her voice and her gestures as she talks to the twins gives her the better kind of beauty. I have to admit. How do *I* look in *her* eyes? With Melissa by my side. Will she even remember my face from her rare visits to see James in the office?

Yes, she does, and looks away, shocked.

Okay. I can understand that. Wouldn't *I?* But we are together in this, Joyce, that we are thinking of each other. What if . . . ?

Driving up here, did Joyce just miss seeing James's latest office fuck coming out of *our* restaurant?

I didn't want this child, Glenda. Carol looked affectionately down at the crown of Melissa's head. I wanted Tim, my firstborn, very much, but with only one of the three possible fathers—James.

What if James had left her for me? The twins would not be swinging, not *be.* Melissa would not be feeding that stray cat the last of her French fries. A juxtaposition so ordinary, it is extraordinarily strange. What if Tim were here and Joyce saw him and wondered, reckoning the time factor? And James, you come into this, too, love of my life. Suddenly, there is the boy who is most probably your son, before the twins. Even just seeing Melissa might make you wonder about the son you know I have. Open your mouth, James, let me swab for DNA, and let's tune in to Eyewitness News at six—film at eleven—to hear the answer. Why can't we all be just one big happy family, the family of man? *One* man? You.

A silly notion, Carol. Who said that? Is that you, Glenda, you of all people?

Who is that man, Mrs. James Marquart? Another F? You are shaking your head, looking my way, scared, he is nodding, turning away.

Seeing Joyce with that man, Carol wondered whether James is father of the twins.

Who was that man talking to you?

Carol had seen James with a woman not his wife, and now his wife talking with a man not her husband in the park, hearing nothing, seeing only the puffs of breath smoke in the freezing air.

Back on the interstate, Melissa in the backseat with that broken toy kalei-doscope, Carol tried to remember exactly what was going on in her own life when her mother shot herself.

She could remember more easily what was going on in her mother's life, exactly, because her mother's life had gone by the clock.

She knew that her own life as a mother—driving an old Oldsmobile, her daughter in the backseat—would give no one watching the slightest indication that she was "of two minds," and what was going on in either one of them.

Just outside Alexandria Bay, she stopped at the grungy service station, parked beside a pickup truck.

"May I have an oil change, please, sir?"

"Hey, Wingnut, guess who's back here already?"

"Weren't you just in here?" Wingnut's outspread hands seemed to ask that question.

"Three months or three thousand miles, whichever comes first. I'm trying to be more responsible."

"Took some long trips, did you?"

"You could say that."

"Why did that man call you Wingnut?"

"That's my name."

"Your own mother named you Wingnut?"

"Melissa . . ."

"Sure. Just like your own mother named you Melissa."

As Wingnut talked, Carol stared at the car as a body. I have not been paying attention to my own body. Not even enough to feel constipated.

"You must run this car to death, Lady."

"Sometimes I think it liked its former owner better."

Father, you used to stroke it, pat it, whistle for it to come to you like it was the Lone Ranger's horse, kick its front tire before lifting the hood or getting in to go. But I'll never let it go. I might even give it a name one of these days.

"An oil change more often would sure make it like you."

Why is he taking three steps toward me, then three steps backward, then repeating the sequence. What is that man trying to say?

"Go ahead. We'll wait. And anything else you think it needs."

"Needs a brand new driver." He seemed to want her to hear what he said to the other guy under the other car down in the bay well.

Her father would have a comeback.

"We'll wait where it's warm, at the Mobil up the highway."

Holding hands, they crossed Highway 12.

"That's his nickname. Wingnut."

"Why didn't he say so?"

"Because you're a kid."

"Yes, that's true. I forget till somebody reminds me."

Another occasion for teaching Melissa how to cross a street, a highway. She was already way ahead of many adults, who almost always strolled or jogged with their backs to the traffic—even pushed their strollers two abreast, oblivious. After she told her that "your grandmother May drilled that into me when I was your age," Melissa caught them every time and reported them to Carol.

And they just go right on doing it, don't they, Glenda? Like the women who leave their windows up, their doors unlocked, even standing open. Did they find your Mercedes locked? Yes.

"Do *you* have a nickname?"

"No."

Do you, Glenda? Does F? Most criminals do. And tattooed slogans and threats and mottos.

As they stood again before Wingnut, stuff from the Mobil station snack bar was *in* them.

"She's done, and humming."

She always cringed when men spoke of inanimate objects—cars, boats, motors, guns—as "she." She had kept meaning to ask one of them why, but so far, had not. "He" is reserved for the one who uses the objects. And yet, Glenda, I don't feel like an object used by the men in my life. I know they do it, but I never feel it. I do feel uneasy. That's the word. Or "disquietude," as my father would say.

Wingnut out of sight, Carol had to keep his face willfully out of her mind as she imagined Glenda looking at F. Carol had not yet clearly seen F's face. Glenda must look into that face, so I must see it with her. But not like Wingnut's. Or any other face I see in Alexandria Bay or in Watertown.

She knew Frank was waiting, just off Church Street on Rock in front of their church. Sure it was safe, she ran the red light and, when she heard the siren and saw flashing red in her rearview mirror, pulled over. He is nice, even sort of fatherly, even though we graduated together. And maybe I want to taunt, punish, Jack. No, I hope that's not in me to do.

"You may pay the fine by mail or appear in court to contest the fine, on that." From childhood, she had told him not to tack "on that" at the end of his sentences, but now was not the time to repeat it. "Have a nice day, Carol."

Had he seen the Watertown traffic ticket on the seat beside her? She put his ticket over the campus cop's.

"He was very nice about it." Melissa seemed glad to be able to say that to her.

Carol looked for the coyote on her rooftree.

Under her roof, in the living room, sat a faintly familiar woman, dressed to kill.

"Jack let me in. and then somebody blew their horn for him, and he took off somewhere, said, 'I leave you to your own devices.'"

"Heard it in a movie once and adopted it as his own."

But Jack at least has a purpose—volunteer fireman—always on call. And now he sails on air over the ice in his rented airboat with all the searchers, led by Thyre Mann, famous forensic anthropologist, body finder, blower of the horn probably.

"He works with me a lot, finds houses for sale in the course of doing his own work. I'm Rita Harrington, Dream House Realty. Jack thought you might be willing to consider an offer on this house."

"Jack seldom thinks before he has a thought. I wouldn't think of selling it. Do you think my father had anything to do with your visit?"

"Not unless perhaps Jack conferred with him."

"No, they never confer. They come at me from separate directions. And now you."

"Sorry to disturb you, Carol. Maybe another time."

"Maybe over my dead body. Oh! Forgive me, Ms. Harrington. I wasn't thinking."

"That was thirty-five years ago, my dear. My brother refused to let me sell it, too. He was afflicted with a terrible nostalgia for this house and that view."

"Do you think the romance of Boldt Castle lured him into becoming a Pearl Poet Scholar and a poet himself?"

"Wayne kept to himself. We did not really know him. You seem to know a good deal about my brother."

"My mother often told me the history of this house."

"Wayne's wife never hesitated to sell, but then she—"

"She—what was *she* like?"

"Absolute zero. Ann was an absolute zero. Not a thought in her head." Never of two minds? "But a good enough wife and mother in her own remote way."

"I hear she was in this very room all alone when it happened."

"Oh, yes. Followed him up here, don't you know. The most audacious thing she ever did, given her absolute helplessness, you name it, but she actually arranged a flight, all by herself. Unbeknownst to me, he had come back to our family house, that I had emptied in an estate sale so I could sell it. Said she heard the shot but thought it was a truck backfiring, thought he had just wandered out on the ice, got lost among the islands, and would turn up any day back home in West Virginia, don't you know. Can you imagine what it was like to find your own brother—I met *yours* once—like that, in a corner of your childhood home, huddled up behind a bush, in a puddle the thawed snow left? Our lilac bush, on the west side."

"I know. At first, our latest stray cat used to go there and stand and look. But now that's where she sleeps, in fair weather. Found her there last week, the day it was suddenly sixty degrees."

Carol saw herself looking for Wayne Harrington's gravestone in Alexandria Bay's three small graveyards.

Or did Rita have him cremated? To remove all evidence?

Was he Catholic, forbidden burial? No, Episcopal, that church that faces the river, across from the clinic.

Buried in the cemetery across from Walton Market or the one for older families, a block north of the highway, huge boulders all around? Or cast to the wind like my mother?

"My mother told me that's why she was able to afford the house. But to her, what happened here was routine, working at the Good Samaritan ER. You keep looking up at that urn on the mantel. Mother's—always sets on that mantel. Empty."

Came to her mind now her appealing to Kenneth Bradley's nostalgia for their good old high-school days to take her up onto the Sky Deck across the river in Canada and leave her alone for a little while with her mother.

When the subzero wind picked up, shrieking around the deck, I opened the urn and sowed the ashes into the waves of wind.

"I'm going to become a nurse. I got a late start."

"Just like your mother." Only, most likely not. "I knew your mother, of course. Sometimes May would share a table with me at Dockside Pub. We liked the French fries, don't you know." She extended her hand, let it hover over Carol's. "You can imagine how shocked I was. And you only nineteen. But you seem to have handled it well over the years."

"That's what they all say. Even my father. Who should know better." Carol cut the pause with a basic question. "What does your husband do?"

"Not every woman needs to be married, don't you know." That set in another pause, cut when Rita stood up. "Well, given my own connection—the family home place and all—can you promise that if you ever do even *consider* selling, it'll be me you call?"

"Absolutely, Rita. Oh, your hands are cold."

"Honey, hands are cold all over the Northeast and all of Canada today."

Rita gone, Carol went over to the window that gave her and her mother and Wayne the best view of Boldt Castle.

Professor Helvy drives his jaunty 2006 Nissan up from Watertown to Alexandria Bay, but he goes over the Intercontinental Bridge to Hart House Bed and Breakfast to talk philosophy with the proprietor—or visit some woman—more often than to see his grandchildren. Maybe it's the house he doesn't want to see. But I feel close to my mother here. And now, since you've been missing, I feel close to Wayne Harrington, too, who was missing, too, for a while, until the snow thawed and his own sister found him that way, his wound self-inflicted.

"I could have taught at Harvard," she had overheard her father explain to a prospective buyer, sneering at himself, a few days before Carol had learned that her mother had willed the house to her and she'd insisted on keeping it, "but our honeymoon in Alexandria Bay—my bright idea—nipped that in the bud. May vowed to spend the rest of her life here, may she rest in peace, and bought this house a year after the nostalgic Pearl Poet scholar shot himself just below that window. Commuting ages the fool who does it, and Watertown has the institution of higher learning closest to Alexandria Bay."

I don't know why Momma left it to me personally and not to my father. She never said anything about it, much less why, and she left no note.

Wanted her daughter to figure it out for herself, I suppose.

I never asked Father, and he never volunteered.

Jack being Jack loved the idea of a free house at the start of a marriage, his first, my second.

In front of her house, two old ladies dawdled, bent over, with a dachshund, car door wide open, in the middle of the street. One of many pickup trucks on the icy street swerved to miss, the women oblivious.

The only house my mother could afford was a house where a poet shot himself outside, where my mother shot herself inside.

Has Wayne Harrington's wife—what's her name? Sorry, I don't know your first name—ever returned, stood outside looking up at the house? Knocked at the front door, the back door, when I was gone, to ask Jack or Tim could she come inside to look around or stand outside and take a photograph? Will I ever see her face to face?

4

Are you somewhere between Watertown and Syracuse, plowing through Nordic Snow Alley that Tug Hill Plateau creates? If you are, both of you are in danger now. Look at it snow!

You notice even how deeply he inhales his cigarette smoke—Suck in. Pause. Spew out.

How he applies the brakes, then brings his alligator boot back.

How he rests his free hand on his knee or on the back of the seat, fingertips almost touching your shoulder. Or the dashboard. Or on the knob of the stick shift. When he takes his hand away, you see the knob is worn and shiny.

How he flexes his shoulders and jerks his neck aside when he speaks, like that southern redneck TV evangelist. And whatever other gestures go with what kind of thing he is saying to you.

Is he telling you things that sound like something he doesn't tell other people? His wife. Does he have a wife? Children? Some of them do. And even go to church regularly. And have friends. And are very friendly. They never fit the sinister image everyone imagines, do they? Well, almost never. Just like us. But I don't think Methodists become killers very often. Maybe not Presbyterians either, what they say you are.

You pay close attention to his gestures, too, and his gestures do run the gamut, especially now that he is talking a blue streak. You know now what not to talk about, and that's good, because you can keep to neutral things and that's good, too. Some words, questions are like triggers on a cocked pistol. Talk is your only weapon, but it's a dangerous weapon.

You notice he tries not to give you information that you can use against him if it comes to that. And you think it's partly because he doesn't *want* to have to make sure you never tell it, don't you?

I try to stay out of trouble, he says, and you try to keep from laughing because you laugh all the time, people tell you they love your laugh, loud but not raucous, still classy, ladylike. Maybe you could say high tone.

Was F ever incarcerated in the corrections facility on Highway 12, between the village of Cape Vincent and the village of Clayton? Incinerated, you mean. Incarcerated, yourself you may as well be.

F still has not made a move. And you have played with him exactly the same level of friendliness you always played in public. A friendliness that made each man feel part of a Glenda circle of friends, but otherwise not inviting anything beyond friendliness. We know that if he begins, he won't, can't stop. We know. Not just you and me, but F knows, too. He has a good relationship with you and will soon have in his hands more money than he has ever had, and even though the sharp edge of an unseen knife and a revolver are the cause of getting both, he knows that touching you improperly will shatter that delicate balance. *We* know.

You are staring at that scar on your shin that you got rock climbing in the Adirondacks before you married anybody. Keep staring at it. You survived the fall, don't forget. Let that scar remind you.

* * *

I need to be with Melissa.

"Tim's playing up at Logan's house."

"I'm going to ask Logan to marry me one of these days."

"Well, let's not get ahead of ourselves. In the meantime, let's you and me go out for supper. Walk down to Riveredge. Be there when the lights first come on at the castle, close up for a change."

As the plump hostess seated them by the windows, a very tall waiter was informing a winter tourist couple that "Alexandria Bay has a 120-day economy. If you can't make it in 120 days, you're dead. So we hustle."

And the rest of the year we *all* play dead.

She dreaded spring, the huge vacation cruisers, and the streets bloated with bloated people pretending to have the time of their lives, the intrusion of the dreary faces of gaiety.

Winter is no pretense, not even for the few winter tourists.

Poised as mother and daughter on the edges of their chairs, Carol and Melissa missed the instant at twilight when the lights first illuminated Boldt Castle. Staring, they inhabited the sight of it.

"This is a drinking town." The docent-like waiter informed a solitary businessman type.

Melissa stood up, as if to see the castle more clearly. "I like the water tower by Hart House, too. Rusty red."

"Don't forget your other favorite tower, across from church."

"I read where Hart Island Tower springs twenty little leaks each year." The waiter seemed to assume they were odd tourists in need of a thrill. "A time bomb about to explode. All the rich houses will drown, except Hart House Bed and Breakfast, maybe, because it sets on a hill." He looked down into Melissa's upturned face. "The Boldt family lived in Hart House while the castle—we call them cottages, why, don't ask *me*—was being built, and then they pushed the house across the ice and named it Hart House, Hart as in stag, and George Charles Boldt, the Prussian who owned the Waldorf-Astoria hotel in New York City, had the island carved, so goes the legend, into a heart and dubbed it Heart Island."

"Yes, we know. Don't we, Mother?"

"Yes, we do, yes, we do. But thank you."

"Do you want me to tell you about our dessert specials?"

"Don't it remind you of Heidelberg Schloss?" the winter tourist asked his wife, or whoever might really be listening.

"It's our Wine and Chocolate Weekend, too, so you may take your pick."

"Why not both?"

She looked at her husband.

He shrugged.

The couple fell silent, listening to some know-it-all behind Carol's table.

"Do you think the grass is greener in Plattsburgh or some damn place? Alexandria Bay is not just here, Buster, but everywhere you go, so to speak, and also literally. How about Alexandria, Egypt? Good ol' humdrum Alexandria, Egypt, right up there with good ol' home sweet home Alexandria, Virginia.

Getting out of town won't get you anywhere, Buster, but right back into Alexandria Bay, upstate New York, unless you intend to become like Alexander the Great, who went everywhere in the known world, leaving behind city after city that he named Alexandria, and kicked the bucket at Jesus' same age. Get my drift?"

Eager to get beyond earshot of mister loudmouth, waiting to pay, Carol tried and failed to turn a deaf ear to two waiters talking loudly by the doorway to the dining area.

"They told her, no, it's not till the twenty-sixth, which she said, 'Shit! I'll be in Prague on the twenty-sixth.' Imagine that. Ninety-five years old and walks like a high school athlete, and down that flight of steps from Bonny Castle porch she goes, the sleeves of her red robe fucking flapping like a bird, down to the bank, drops that robe, off that bank she goes, naked as your bald head, wades without a care in the world into the water where they broke open the ice this morning and swims out and into the current of the Saint fucking Lawrence River, man. Can you feature that?"

"And that's her standing there?"

Robed in red, a tall, vigorous woman, gray hair hanging long down her back, stood at the elevator, impatiently push-pushing the button. You, Glenda, forty years from now.

"Sure as the world is. Eating a piece of chocolate. I hope that's me when I hit ninety-five. Come to find out, she's this famous novelist and foreign correspondent that was once married to Ernest Hemingway."

"No kidding. What about that? Hey, man, who's Ernest Hemingway?"

Carol drove out of the Riveredge parking lot and over to Church Street and uphill and across Highway 12 to defunct BAY DRIVE-IN THEATRE, WHERE THE MOVIES MEET THE STARS.

"Well, here we are."

"It's no movie because it's too cold."

"But this morning, you said you wanted to go to the drive-in movie, so here we are."

Melissa released herself from her child restraint, crawled over the back of the front seat, nestled up to Carol, leaned forward, peering through the windshield where snow was sticking. She turned on the wipers.

"That's better."

"What's showing?" Nothing on the screen, everything was imaginable.

"Can't you see? It's *The Wizard of Oz* just before her shoes turn red."

How blessed I am, Glenda, to have Melissa. And you.

But *you* have only F. At the moment.

A penny for your thoughts.

What thoughts? F sneers at the very idea.

You look like you are deep in thought.

I have never been deep in anything but trouble in my whole life.

Well, I can imagine your having a good time, from time to time.

Imagine all you want to, that don't make it so.

Think, think back. You are just a kid and life has not yet taken you by the neck and you are, what? Listening to the question, he is sticking his arms straight out, flexing his shoulders. You are totally absorbed in playing with one particular toy, happily oblivious of the world around you. Remember?

How did you know?

Everybody has that one moment, at least that one moment, that moment they never forget, that moment they treasure, cherish for the rest of their lives, that moment they remember when they think their lives have been more wasteful than not.

Yeah. Me, too. I had one, too.

Will you tell me?

No.

Well, I'm a good listener.

No, I mean, I forgot.

Oh.

Oh, Glenda, you shouldn't have said, 'Oh.'

Then look to the future.

Yes.

What future? Now you see me, now you don't.

I see you with a good share of the money, pursuing your dreams in some foreign town that has a sparkling sandy beach.

Dreamland, Lady. When I get the money in my two hands, we can talk about it. You go your way, I go mine, huh?

No. I didn't mean that. If we part after we withdraw the money, it will be your choice.

Yes, Glenda, talk to him that way. He may suspect you are doing mind games on him but enjoy it enough to play along.

* * *

Jack held it up the way he used to hold up a dirty diaper. "You got this ticket for what?"

"Red light violation."

"Ran a red light, with our daughter in the car? Frank should have arrested you instead. Teach you a lesson. It's not enough you got a ticket for 'parking' last week. What? Parking cross-eyed? What were you doing to get a ticket for parking?"

"They do not allow you to park on the side of the highway unless you are fixing a tire or sticking your head under the hood." I am trying to tell him what I was doing over the river in Canada last week but, Glenda, I guess nobody ever really listens when they feel certain you are spinning a web of lies. Do *you* ever?

Knowing how predictable he would be, Carol told him "She was a woman cop."

"Just as I thought. Otherwise, I would have gotten a call to come bail you out." Listen to how calm he sounds, even though he's speaking through clenched teeth. "Parking violations are one thing, but worse, you got a ticket for speeding a few weeks before that? With my daughter in the car."

"Your daughter was not in the car, your son was babysitting her."

"Since when is Tim old enough? And who, pray tell, was babysitting you that you was speeding?"

"I do better without the insults."

"I do better without carving a few hundred dollars worth of flesh out of my hardworking ass and paying sky-high insurance monthly."

Carol laughed. Carol realized she was laughing the way Glenda would laugh.

Jack looked at her as if he didn't recognize the laugh.

She tried to laugh like herself, but sounded like an idiot.

"One other thing while we are at it. I hit a deer."

"Say that again."

"I said, I hit a deer—today."

He let that soak in, as if hoping it would vanish. "Well, around here, who has *not* hit a deer, once or twice in his life?" He was straining to overcome the shock.

"Oh, good. I was afraid I was the only one who ever hit a deer on the Jefferson Community College campus."

"I hate to say it, but you are definitely a menace to society."

He's right, of course. I am sometimes recklessly impulsive, going to the lighthouse in zero, snow-blowing weather, no snow mask, my child in tow.

One time I put Melissa in a rowing skiff my brother-in-law let me borrow, to go over to Sunken Rock Lighthouse, just to touch it, but I suddenly realized I was a grown-up and did not actually set out.

Another time, I drove alone to Chippewa Bay and watched the men drive out on the ice. We lose at least one truck each year, I heard one of the men tell a man who dangled about like a winter tourist. With that information in my ears, I eased my Oldsmobile out onto the ice among the men, and they looked at me like I was about to sink us all.

From orbiting the house to shake off his anger, Jack came back in, tracking fresh snow. "Your father stopped by the construction site in La Fargeville this afternoon."

"What in the hell for?"

"He asked me what your average day was like." Carol classified his tone as a "furthermore" tone that proved by implication what he had declared when he walked out.

"*You* tell *me*."

"What you do each day, your routine, and how you deviate."

"What did you tell him?"

"That you are certainly nothing like my mother, as far as being a house-wife."

"Did you list my 'deviations'?"

"'Deviations' was his word, not mine, his professor word. Deviates are like perverts, ain't they?"

"Did you *list* them?"

"I told him, Ask her, if you really want to know."

"What did he say to that?"

"Will you stop quizzing me! He just said you seemed beside yourself."

"'Beside myself'?" She could ask her father why he sought out Jack, but she already knew why people might think her recent behavior patterns deviated from the norm.

Her father's behavior wasn't quite the same as before either.

And look at Jack.

But look at Melissa. Same old Melissa.

Look at Tim. Well, we'll see. Shut up in his room with that put-on angry-sounding music and the feelings and thoughts such music inspires.

F's behavior is not at all what it was with the six maybe seven other women, much less his own family.

The only one really behaving the way you would expect is *you,* Glenda.

So I need not worry too much about my own behavior. I am glad, though, that my father is keeping an eye on me.

Did he keep an eye on *you,* mother?

My mother. I once trailed along after my mother the way Melissa does with me. Odd to think of it that way. Except we never roamed the streets in an old Oldsmobile, "Wearing down the treads," Wingnut says. Time for new tires. Shell out, Jack. He comes and goes. How are *his* treads?

My father's a walker, leaves his Nissan parked at school sometimes just to walk, walks from the heights between one class and another, down through the valley and up Thompson Park heights. I sometimes pass him as he lopes along. "Why ride when you can just as well walk?" I like seeing him walk across the quad. Or does he have a girlfriend at last and walk to see her? Dad, do you have a girlfriend? What a question. I hope he does. But *does* he?

Did you have a secret lover, Mother? Some doctor perhaps? No. No, she didn't. That wasn't it. It was something else. What was it? Nobody can ever say for sure, they say. And you, Glenda? Wait. It's the TV.

"We don't have the man and woman power here to search the islands, so they are coming in from all over, FBI included. With over a thousand islands to search, it's like looking for victims or survivors from a tsunami."

"They called me to come in and give a swab." Jack was already out of the room, responding to Thyre's horn, both late for the gathering of the search party.

"Tra-la," as my Irish mother used to say.

You're on ABC news now, Glenda, but partly because the searchers around here just found the seventh victim's body on an island in the Lost Channel area of the Thousand Islands, posed in an elegant chair facing the front door of one of the icebound island cottages, her throat cut. Kathy Donovan, 35, a Watertown advertising executive. I'm promising her now not to forget her name.

DNA has now been taken from the mouths of thousands of men.

Will they call in all the men in your life, Carol, past and present?

She stuck her finger in her mouth and looked at it.

I'm beside myself, my mother said, staring into the fireplace, not even slightly moving.

Was Wayne Harrington "beside himself" when he shot himself?

After they found him, his widow was *beside* herself, so says Rita.

Does being beside yourself increase the population, or are you simply here, instead of over there?

Imagining that scene, her father telling Jack, "Carol seems beside herself," she had a terrifying sensation of being beside herself at a level deeper than cliché.

On her mother's side, both her grandparents, she was told, were gone when she was born, and no relatives.

"Was my mother an orphan, Father?"

"I am taking the fifth. Any answer may change your life. I refuse to take the responsibility for that. As your father, I advise you to live the life you have."

She wished she could go over his head to her grandfather Helvy, but he died when she was six. And her grandmother Helvy a year later.

So, I cannot turn to my German immigrant grandfather Helvy, from Warfield, Bavaria.

I cannot turn to my Irish immigrant grandmother Helvy, a Reilly from Galway.

I cannot turn to my unknown grandfather Sullivan, from God knows where.

I cannot turn to my anonymous grandmother Sullivan, from some unknown godforsaken place.

When I finally meet you, Glenda, in the flesh, I will tell you about my mother.

Her mother. When she saw her mother in memory, she was just as real as her father standing in front of her now, except when she remembered something her father did or said. Knowing she would see him again made him more real than her mother. Maybe that makes the difference between the dead and the living, knowing you will see the living again, later in the day, tomorrow, or soon, or eventually.

She lay in bed, grieving, remembering her first sight of Bill, the back of his head, just ahead of her in Intro to Earth Sciences at Syracuse University her freshman year. When Bill stood up, Carol had seen that his ass was lovely. A few weeks later, she was stroking it, a pure delight. Other young men were otherwise attractive, each in a very different way, as if, she realized, she were sampling an array of possibilities, but, no, they were simply there, unsought, week after week, until Thornton the frat boy loomed above her, dick dangling, and stepped on the wrist of her left hand when she tried to get up.

Alone on a bicycle, she put the winter and the mountains of Greece like a wall between herself and the frat boy—*all* men, including Bill.

When she returned, tan and strong, she and Bill argued about the wall that still remained, a fabric of intangibles.

"Even so, I want to marry you, Carol."

Even now, she did not know why she held back, because she liked Bill so much she supposed she must also love him, and, in domestic confines, the wall might gradually crumble.

Then Bill announced, "Bush is sending me to chase Saddam Hussein out of Kuwait." But the president failed to warn him to be on the lookout for rusty nails, that if you step on one and your foot gets infected. . . .

The image of herself standing by Bill's grave, holding her mother's hand on one side and Bill's father's hand on her other side, was getting clearer and clearer, when—I heard the shot, Glenda, and then another. The first shot shattered a jar of her fig preserves, so her mother fired the second into her mouth. Hold on. I'm confusing one time with another.

The house was left empty for two years, except for her mother's lost spirit—and Wayne Harrington's—while Carol found an apartment in Watertown, dropped out of Syracuse mid-semester, looked for and found a job, working for James Marquart, lawyer, and met and, with painful hesitation, married Gordon Masterson, a civil engineer ten years her senior.

Too late, I realized that the source of the pain was my love for James. I felt more married to James, who was married, than to Gordon, who sensed the mistake we had made within the first month. But not until I confessed my affair with James a year later did Gordon divest himself of me.

The weekend the divorce became final, I met Jack in a bar during a nostalgic visit back to Alexandria Bay. He was like firm earth under my feet, until James, within the same month, reacted to the news of my pregnancy by declaring everlasting love for his pregnant wife. I told all three, including Gordon, who had sweetly seduced me, so to speak, in that same month, just before our divorce became final. None of them wanted to know who the father was. Now Tim and I will have to deal with the mystery someday.

So, you see, Glenda, when we finally sit down together in Watertown's classiest restaurant, it will be a lot to ask of you, to listen to all these circumstances of my early adulthood. I feel as if I am always turning around and around, merely to get my bearings. So when I wonder where you are now, I know how you must feel. It's the damned not knowing, as my father tells me my grandfather loved to say.

* * *

Standing on her front porch, Carol watched the St. Lawrence's swift channel current break up the ice between the shore and Boldt Castle.

Here we are in the middle of nowhere, and doesn't it remind you of those grim *Life* magazine photos of the hills and mountains and squalid houses of eastern Kentucky? By the road and off up among rocks and winter trees, rocks in the snow, five in a row, fantastic shapes, frequent large rocks, brown, red, outcroppings, you see many abandoned stone and wood houses, and you feel in yourself what the word expresses, "abandoned." But more than rot and fire-prone wood, in yourself you feel, deep down, enduring stone.

"Nice" is the word for Hammond Village, desolation all around, and the word seems to mock you.

Out there in the snow stand horses, oblivious, noses rooting into the snow for green grass blades.

F gets back into the driver's seat and backs up. It's kind of a long way back up to the road, and he seems to be showing you how well he does that. You know how they are about stuff like that. I never could. Oh, but I bet *you* could. But don't compete. Let *him* do it.

I remember that very tree. Stark. But I stopped to look at it that time I got lost on those rough roads back in there. Draped in winter-withered vines.

I am doing all I can now, Glenda, but what about *before?* And what about *after?* Well, I assume your life was good when you were free, and will be good when you are free again.

But you know and I know that I know nothing, the same way I know next to nothing about my own life. I'm a stranger here myself.

And now you are at a crossroads.

Which way will he go? Further east? And if so, further south to Gouverneur or north to the Ogdensburg area again or direct east to Canton? Or back toward Highway 12 and the briar thicket on the river bank between Alexandria Bay and Chippewa Bay? Whichever, *he* knows what he is doing. Killing time, knowing that the energy of the hunt dwindles and the focus of it scatters, but that the hunt never strays into these desolate places.

My six-year-old is calling me to help her out of the tub, and my eleven-year-old has already turned himself over to heavy metal or punk rock, or whatever, and it's far, far too loud for human ears to bear. If I tell him to smother it a little or shut it down, he will. Why don't I tell him to do that? What holds me back sometimes?

* * *

WATCH FOR FALLEN ROCK.

F stops at the Oxbow Country Store. Get a fix on what you see. ICE to the left, by the door, OPEN to the right, then BUDWEISER, then a mailbox. The view out your side window is striking, that white church, bold steeple, at the end of the one street.

"Please, while you're in there, get me a pocket comb."

Run, Glenda, jump out and run.

No, don't. We don't know how fast he can run and how accurate his aim is or how much he cares if they chase him or even catch him.

F comes out, holding a bag.

Out of Oxbow, F turns onto another road on no map and gets lost.

Got lost one time in Lost Channel below Ivy Lea.

Don't ask if that was when he was looking for a place to leave one of the other women. Sorry. You don't need *me* to tell you *that*.

On the road, he shakes open the bag and pulls out a quart of Hershey White House cherry-vanilla ice cream (my favorite), can't open the lid, stuck so fast.

Want some help?

No, I got it.

Steering over the rough rutted road with his left hand, he has to use his teeth to get the flap up, then it's too hard for the plastic spoon, so he chews the cardboard down, gnaws on the cherry vanilla.

When the ice cream gets a little softer, he offers it to you to bite, then lick.

The snow becomes a blizzard, and you two are driving through it, eating ice cream.

You both get cherry-vanilla ice cream all over your faces and hands.

At moments, I feel panicky for my own life simultaneously with yours. I feel guilty for the thought that because he is with you, he is no threat to me.

Search leader Thyre Mann came on TV to announce that the blizzard has postponed the search for you. So no matter how important you are. . . .

* * *

Glenda stopped the Oldsmobile impulsively.

"Why are we in the boneyards today?"

"Cemeteries. Well, yes, boneyard."

"Or rock cemeteries. More rocks than people. Did you ever count them all?"

Here I am, Glenda.

"No, but I might sometime."

The policewoman spokesperson said again that Glenda Hamilton still has not been included among the Daylight Serial Killer's victims because no one has found her body.

I feel like calling 911—or I suppose it would be the special tip line—to tell them that they never will find your body until you die of old age and they come to the funeral home during family visitation hours and look down into your face, posed on a bed of pearl-white silk.

"The Valley of Ten Thousand Smokes in Alaska." Tim stood a moment between Carol and the television news. "When I grow up, that's where I'm going. To live. I hate the Thousand Islands!" Sounded more like an announcement than a declaration uttered in anger.

"'Duly noted,' as your grandfather would say. Now, do me a favor, make me a list of *all* the things you hate. I really want to know. Will you?"

Tim glared at her.

"Please? For your mother?"

Tim did a smart military about-face, left the room.

They speak to me from another room, and when I ask them to repeat what they said, they always sigh deeply before they speak again. Maybe I'm not a good listener, or maybe that's how it is in all households, or most, or some, mine, at least. Oh, I don't really know about other households. I'm not complaining exactly.

Everything Jack was doing and saying and not saying intimated that he was on the verge of asking for it or initiating it. Feeling a quaint, faint sense of wifely obligation, she displayed herself on the bed provocatively. Before his head hit the pillow, she slipped her hand into the slit of his boxers and plopped it, partially erect, into her mouth. He likes it best when I have to dig into his jocks or pull down his briefs. But this will do.

Sometimes lately I feel invisible. I avoid the mirrors, afraid I won't see anything. Then sometimes I go to the mirror in the bathroom to make sure I can. But mirrors that I just happen to pass, showing my face, distract me from you, so I avoid them as a rule. You and the young women were so visible, you caught his eye, and the profilers say he probably followed you for days or weeks first—to nail down your routine, except for you, you he took on impulse because I saw him already standing there when you showed up. He listens to them talk and watches them mingle with other people, people he has to look out for when he finally decides the new one is utterly alone. He is invisible too. That's why you didn't see him.

Tim showed up suddenly at her bedside. "It's finished."

"The list?"

"Yes."

He stood so stiff, she snapped on the lamplight, rousing, but not waking, Jack.

"No, sit by me while I go over it. . . . Long isn't it?" She looked at Tim's face. Shock. A set look of shock. "I know. . . . Well, now you can pay a little more attention to things to love. And no need to make another list. Goodnight." She snapped off the lamplight.

Tim stood stiff by the bed a full minute longer. He turned slowly and left the bedroom, leaving the door open behind him.

Everyone fast asleep always makes me feel I am alone in the house. Not that I like being alone in this house, walking in the dark from room to room.

Remember the man they found somewhere who had lived in a crawlspace under a house in the suburbs for ten years and nobody in the house knew it till "the man of the house" saw him on the news, accused of swiping his favorite cookies from a convenience store? And him clean-shaven and neatly dressed. Sorted mail in the Post Office. These are publicly reported things you and I once shared over the years, Glenda. You know, if I was a man, do you suppose that man might have been me?

I get to looking around at things, and things seem to stand out and demand my attention, distract me from concentrating on you.

Not just that damned bird clock that sings a different bird song each hour that I got in a garage sale and that Jack says proves I'm a nut case, even though I think he likes it. I think he thinks it's woodsy or something, although he wouldn't even yell at a deer—certainly not shoot a dove. Fish, yes. I don't hate it. But sometimes it's a little unnerving. You forget it's there, and suddenly it takes over your whole life for a few seconds. One of these days I will get enough of it and get up on a chair and take it down off the wall from over the refrigerator and put it in a box for Goodwill Industries.

Even the new refrigerator—TO DO magnetized to the door—seems to demand that I look at it—a big avocado man. I have never had a garage sale. Maybe one of these days. You wouldn't even notice these things, Glenda, you are always on the move, doing things, at home even, and then out in the big wide world. But sometimes I feel just as inert as that refrigerator.

The TV set too. Sometimes I just have to turn its face to the wall. One time he came in and found it that way and said, See, that's what I mean, over his shoulder, as he and the boy went on into the kitchen to open the refrigerator, which is what he always does when he comes in, like some men kiss their wife at the door.

F was already there on the porch of the fog house when I got to the lighthouse, and I'm alive, aren't I? Oh, oh, and so are you. We can be thankful for that. I'm blessed I have you to look out for every minute of the day. Even as I am doing my wifely, motherly duties, or prowling the streets in that old car, I am seeing and hearing you crystal clear. I have more energy now because I need it to keep you going, but then I am much more tired at night than before, exhausted, and go to sleep with your face in the mirror, in my mind, like on PAUSE on the DVD.

5

You look at F's hands.

You look down at your own hands.

You look up, and he is looking at your face. He sees your face but cannot see his own.

You cannot see the face he is looking at. Your own face.

Glenda, this is the way we are made. We see others but cannot see what they see, our own face. I see this for the first time, even though human beings have always lived since the creation with this fact all their lives, taken it at face value, as they say. I think this is a shocking revelation, Glenda. Don't you think? Forget mirrors and standing water and other reflectors, even eyes that look at you. Even lovers' eyes. Have you ever even tried to see your own face in the naked lens of the eyes of a person who is looking at you?

I must stop thinking about that. No, it is not even a thought in my mind, but a feeling, a nausea in my gut.

I would tell my father, but he might laugh at me. And then again, he might not.

My husband is yelling. That's not like him.

He's yelling at my son. "Keep your hands off my computer!"

He doesn't have to hit him to hurt him.

Tim ran out of the house, whimpering.

Not to *me*. Just away from *him*.

Jack slammed the doors to the walk-in closet shut.

Without tossing his habitual farewell over his shoulder, "I leave you to your own devices," he shot out the back door.

Is that Jack's father coming up the front steps?

"Carol, I came by because I'm worried about Jack." Jack's father held the tea saucer in both hands.

"What is it?"

"He's not himself lately. I thought you might know why. Or rather *if*."

"No, nothing I know of."

"You know what I think?"

"No."

"That all this business about the Daylight Serial Killer has finally got to him."

"How so?"

"I can't put my finger on it. He is so sensitive."

"Sensitive?"

"Yeah. Well, you know better than anybody how sensitive he is."

Carol barely opened her mouth, enough of a yes for *his* sake.

"Always been that way. Just ask his mother."

"I will. I mean, yes, I see."

"Plus, any man would worry about getting swabbed for no good reason and having it get out. Even if you're one of the searchers, like Jack. Anyways, what do *I* know? All *I* know is insurance."

"Yes, you sure know that, don't you?"

"Thanks for talking with me about it, Carol."

"You are certainly very welcome."

Gently, she shut the door. The door took his place.

Well, maybe he *is* sensitive. More than I can tell.

What do *I* know? Not enough, I guess.

Looking forward to riding in the car with Melissa, Carol hoped to hear some of her wit.

When Melissa looked up from the array of her toys on the floor, she seemed to shrink back from the sight of Carol in the doorway of her room.

Carol sang the phrase from Willie Nelson's song "On the Road Again." Melissa obediently stood up and started walking. "Don't forget your kaleidoscope."

"I don't want it."

"How come?"

"It's broken."

"It's *been* broken."

"I know." Melissa walked out of her room past Carol.

The old Oldsmobile sits out there in the fog like a guilty witness waiting to testify.

"Oh, look, Melissa, a strange dog on the marina."

"She walks like she's wounded."

She saw Frank's patrol car turn off Church onto Walton. Knowing he would pass her house again later and she would *not* be standing at the window watching him go by made her feel a presentiment of her own death.

"And before you know it, we are on the outskirts of Watertown." But why?

"I'm not surprised."

She knew her ex-husband from the back—Gordon, walking along the highway, briskly, like a man carrying a gas can, but he was not carrying a gas can.

She was sure he had run out of gas, the way he used to. Driving the latest-model BMW but walking it, like any wage earner who rides the needle down to empty as a general rule right on through the last fumes, hopeful gambler. Bridge builder adrift on a becalmed highway on the outskirts.

She kept going, hoping he didn't see her. I harbor no ill will.

She stopped, waited.

"Need a lift?"

"No. But thank you." He walked on past the car.

Carol passed him.

She drove around the block, into the past.

I'll bet you're the kind of man who plays golf every chance he gets.

Golf? Hell, no. You are looking at a man who loves to hunt, fish, play a mean game of handball, and I look for a boxing partner whenever I feel I am about to stomp somebody for unfairly crowding me.

You are bad news, Carol remembered thinking. But, but, you are looking into my eyes. He never spoke in my presence without looking straight into my eyes, Glenda, with a tenderness that said, Don't listen to all that macho talk. He's just a forty-year-old man who is too much aware that he has only five more years until he becomes obsessed with being middle-aged and totally gray. He knows too well what he thinks the world expects of him as a successful man, specifically a civil engineer, and what endeared him to her was that he seemed oblivious to the fact that such a man does not look into a woman's eyes with a true male tenderness and then not stop looking when she begins to talk.

Seeing Gordon still walking up ahead, she cruised up behind him, alongside him.

"Get in."

He got in, without speaking.

"Melissa, meet Gordon. He's the one that planted Gordon's tree."

"We call it Gordon's tree."

"I forgot all about that tree."

"What else did you forget?"

"I get the feeling *you* haven't forgotten *any*thing. I've become an architect also. Take a look at my latest building as we go by. See it?"

"It doesn't look finished."

"It will be. Soon."

She drove over one of his bridges, the one they crossed on their first date.

"We couldn't be crossing Black River at this point, were it not for me."

"How so?"

"I built it. Remember?"

She stopped.

"Not here. I moved. Two blocks up."

She stopped for a red light. "I passed our old house on Flower Avenue the day before I had surgery."

"Here's where I leave you. Next time you see me, please pass me by."

Melissa is probably wondering how I feel about that parting shot.

The traffic cop who gave Carol the ticket for hitting the deer, his motorcycle parked at the busiest intersection in town, in the circle, among the public statues, was waving a funeral cortege through. Or maybe not.

There's such a thing as a generic cop, I suppose. Well, then, how about generic housewives, former nursing students?

He looks like he feels he is belted into manhood, armed. How many men and how many women on the face of the earth feel belted in and armed, ready to defend those of us who are not? How many, many more are belted in and armed, ready to kill as many of us as they can before they are killed? Should I ask him, Glenda? It's not his fault, but should I ask him anyway, since it is he who wears the shiny belt and the gun on his hip? Knowledge, my father never tires of saying, is power.

The third time going past him on Washington, she got the cop's attention. She waved, and he seemed to recognize her, so she went around the Augustus St. Gaudens statue of turn-of-the-century governor Roswell Pettibone Flowers, right hand upraised like a diffident traffic cop, a fourth time and slowed, her window down, and beckoned him.

At her window, he smiled, recognizing her. "Going awful slow, aren't you?"

"Thanks to you. Can I thank you over a cup of coffee?"

"Sure." Hiking up his gun belt, he saw Melissa, alert in the backseat. "But, actually, I have three more hours at this post, then I have to report to the pistol range, and after that . . ." He shrugged.

"Check you another time." Writing down her number again for the traffic cop, she imagined Frank's voice calling, asking to see her in some secluded place.

Driving on, she realized she had given him her number on the back of her TO DO list.

Where am I?

"Melissa, can you tell your mother where we are at the moment?"

"Don't ask *me*. You're the mother." Does she think I'm ribbing her?

"So I am."

Approximately, where are we? Oh, yes, now I see where we are.

Cruising by the hospital where Dr. Christina Trenton would perform surgery on her breast again Monday, she wondered, Did you by chance work with my mother?

That's my father's and mother's old high school, Glenda. Good old Watertown Senior High School.

For all I know, that might have been your high school, too, Glenda.

She turned back to Washington Street—we have a Washington Street in Alexandria Bay, too—and parked in the Hospital House of the Good Samaritan lot.

The lobby was very compact, a series of lighthouse photographs on the walls, evoking a feeling of comfort. She was glad to see that an excellent history of the hospital, with old and new photographs, lined the walls, to learn that it was originally a Trinity and Grace Episcopal Project, 1881, the new hospital built in 1973, on the site of the old one, part of which is adjacent, where Carol had her operation. Lump under her arm, axillary node, afraid they would nick an artery, and did, keeping her three days. And where she will have her second, in and out on the same day.

They had remodeled the cafeteria to make it look pleasant.

In the chapel, tiny as a playhouse, the Bible was open to Romans 7:24.

"O wretched man that I am! Who shall deliver me from the body of this death?"

She opened it at random to "but thou merry—" shut it and turned away to look for the elevator.

On the third floor, she asked, "Did you ever work with May Helvy?"

"May who?"

"Helvy. She was a nurse here about ten years ago."

"Nursing takes a toll on a person. I'm much younger than I look. I was in high school ten years ago."

Younger than I am, by a few years.

"Oh."

"Why do you ask?"

"She was my mother."

"Helen, this lady's asking about her mother. May Helvy, is that right?"

"Yes."

"Well, if it isn't little Carol Helvy. Your mother was my head nurse."

"Helen is head nurse now."

"Good to see you again, Helen. I didn't recognize you at first."

"I haven't seen you since you were a young thing."

"And right here with me is another young thing. Say hello, Melissa, to your grandmother's friend."

"Hello."

"This was her desk?"

"This is the head nurse's desk, yes, was then, still is."

"My mother's going to be head nurse one of these days. . . . Or an astronaut."

"Did you know Dr. Hamilton?"

"Who didn't—doesn't. Thank God, he is still with us. What a fine man he is, maybe you could even say a great man."

"Hear, hear."

"Like anybody, he has his little faults, but . . ."

"We all just pray God he will recover, but medically, we know he can't."

"I only hope nobody has to tell him that his wife is—."

"Well, don't rule out her showing up alive."

"Well, now, we all know better than that, don't we?"

"Well, if we all can be of one mind, all think about her, see her, listen to her, and talk to her, we can save her."

"Come again?"

"She's alive, and she needs us all to talk to her. Just talk to her."

"Would you like a glass of water?"

"No, thank you. I am fine. I am just fine the way I am, maybe a little beside myself. Thank you. Thank you."

Forgive them, Glenda. They don't understand. Death is always at their door. They have to put their hands on people to believe in life. Their hands minister hour by hour, day by day. . . . Like me talking to you, seeing you, listening to you, almost breathing *with* you, almost *for* you, our very heartbeats in sync. Forgive them, please.

Carol felt her body, her mother's spirit, fading back into the hallway, away from the nurse's station, until she was in the elevator, empty, going up. Then down, surrounded by a family, one, two, three, four, weeping.

What "little faults," Glenda? Little to them, big to you? Or ones you do not know about? I hear only your husband's labored breathing, the shock of sudden pain, his unheard plea for a nurse and her needle. I am tormenting you. Forgive me.

You are keeping the image of your husband, robust, as he was, clear. Like those other women, he is struggling to stay alive, but cancer is a killer no one can placate. As the smoker himself may one day come to know. You and your husband and now *I* know. F himself and others like him are a different kind of cancer. There he is, sudden, like cancer, in our lives.

No, no, no. Stop it. Let's move on to something we can do something about. Talk. Talk to him. Words are actions that keep F from taking action.

What can I say?

Anything. Anything to keep his mind from fixing upon taking action.

Tell me, F. Who do you root for?

Nothing and nobody. Who says I have to root for something?

That is a good question. Somebody always wins and somebody always loses. So what's the point in rooting?

And the answer, Lady, is no damn point. I never played and I never watched, so what does that make me?

Interesting. I root for the Red Sox, but, as you say, no point in that.

You probably root for Beethoven, too.

Yes, and even the Beatles.

Oh, yeah?

And Hank Williams.

Your Cheating Heart. Did you ever have a cheating heart?

Not to speak of.

Not to speak of. Well, well, well. Now we know.

And you?

Let's stick with you. I never sat and listened to a woman like you before, so keep talking, about anything.

Anything? My daughters?

Not really. Family talk is boring. Give me something I ain't never heard before.

Oh. Well, let's see. I love Rodin. You've seen *The Thinker* before, haven't you?

The statue of the man sitting with his fist under his chin? Thinking.

And everybody wonders what he's thinking about. The idea that we all have that statue in common appeals to me.

How come?

One of many bonds we all share. Like the Mona Lisa.

With the smile. And what is *she* thinking about?

Or Whistler's Mother for that matter.

Or you. How about you, Lady?

It would be better if he called you Glenda.

I'm thinking you and I have many things in common that would never occur to us if we didn't talk as we're talking now.

Talk is cheap. But I guess not from you, you being rich. You laugh, but I mean it. Your talk is rich. Keep at it.

It's not that I don't like TV, too. I have my favorite shows. Want to know which ones?

Not really. TV makes me feel bad.

Forget TV. Forget family. Let's think about the moon and the stars and rivers and trees.

Careful, Glenda.

I used to lay on my back in my back yard when I was little and look up at the stars and get up and look at them upside down through my legs, and lightning bugs. I liked to be more with stars than with people.

See, that's another thing in everybody's life. The stars and fireflies. Let's you and me get out of the truck and do that. Look up at the stars.

Very dangerous, Glenda. But now you have to, but you lie down first, don't hesitate. Fearless.

You look up at him as he lies down beside you, keeping snow between you. Don't talk.

The silence feels safe.

You pray he does not reach his hand over and touch you.

The ground turns too cold, and you both get up in the same moment.

He looks at you as if you have suddenly appeared and he doesn't know what to make of you.

He goes behind a boulder to piss in the snow.

It's terrible to be treated courteously by a man when you know he might kill you at any moment, just because he can, whether he really wants to or not, if not by plan by impulse. Like a gentleman. In the eyes of a gentleman, you are there and not there.

I told the guy at work, I don't like your attitude toward me, and he says, what attitude you talking about anyway, and I says, that attitude right there, like you think you better than me. Better than you? Of course, I *am* better than you. Everybody's better than anybody else. Do you know what he meant? Because *I* don't. Anyway, he's not the only one. People are like that. They won't leave you alone. You try to talk to them and they give you those looks. Know what I mean? I mean, you take it and you take it and then you feel like you can't take it anymore. It's like they got you surrounded and you got to fight your way out. Know what I mean? I mean, it ain't easy. Never has been for me, not since I was little. Know what I mean?

Try to remember, though, that they have all looked between their legs up at the stars and the moon, upside down in their backyards. Even in Asia. It's almost a human imperative. A given. I mean, you know what I mean.

I know what you mean, without the million-dollar words, I get it. It's just that—No, I never thought of it that way. Everybody doing it the way I did it. In the back yard.

And when *we* looked at the stars together, didn't it make you feel like you and I are not such strangers?

You wouldn't be playing me, would you?

It's a fact, or it's not a fact.

It's a fact. Right.

I was there at the lighthouse.

That's a fact, you were. And I was there before you showed up.

I was there because my mother used to take me there for picnics.

Like you said.

And you?

I don't know. I can't say why I happened to be just right there.

Are you as sleepy as I am?

Probably, but I can't know that for sure, can I?

Close your eyes and don't talk.

You wonder whether he has closed his eyes or is he looking at you through his lashes. He doesn't talk. Is that a good sign or not?

Melissa is asking me, Where is God? I told her, Everywhere.

Even under my bed?

Yes, but also *over* your bed, hovering.

Oh, tell him to go away.

You tell him.

But I'm just a little girl.

He listens to little girls, too.

Same as boys?

Yes.

Same as daddies?

Yes.

Maybe I'll tell him it's okay for him to hover if he wants to.

Good decision.

Carl, I wish I could come rescue you, but I can't.

Oh, yeah, Carol, well, how about Melissa?

No, she will grow up to be like you, Glenda.

Tim. I must rescue Tim. From what? From Jack? From a life misspent in Alexandria Bay? From me and the way my mind works?

James, forgive me. I could have saved you, but to do that, I would have to be born again, and live my life over in a different way. If I wish I could save *you*, why not your wife? Is she not deserving?

Save? Rescue? From what? That's the most difficult question of all to answer, the first question that leads us to all the other questions and answers. Isn't that so, F? Is that right, Glenda?

Carol used a public pay phone at a Shell station to call Dream House Realty and ask for Rita.

"What did your brother think of Alexandria Bay?"

"Wayne loved the Thousand Islands."

"Just wondering."

I walked the same halls he did, sat in the same classrooms, looked out the same windows?

In the house again, she imagined Rita's brother standing at the window, looking out at Boldt Castle on Heart Island, and crossed the room to stand beside him.

"Wayne, why did my mother shoot herself?"

* * *

I wish I could use my husband's computer, but I know it would do no good to ask him to teach me how. I keep fiddling with the one in the public library, but that whole world's so mysterious. I feel like I could take better care of you inside of *that* world, if I typed in everything I have been seeing and hearing and thinking since you first walked up to that observation platform at the light-house. Endow each word with the power of the information superhighway.

Remembering how Jack pored over his user's manual when he first carried it in, she looked all over the house for it, even in hiding places, but found—"Ah, *there* you are!"—only her mother's missing scissors.

Jack's mother called to tell him that she had picked up ten pairs of socks for him cheap at Walmart.

"Tell him to come and get them, will you, please, Carol. He may not like me making choices for him."

Carol assumed Jack's father had shared his concerns about Jack with Mrs. Seabold. "Well, Julia, you know how sensitive he can be."

"I'm not sure I know what you mean." Jack's mother dropped from her brightly attentive mode into her dull oblivious mode.

"Jack. You know what I mean."

"Carol, is he giving you any trouble?"

"Oh, no. I was just referring to how sensitive he is."

"Oh. Yes. Well. . . . And how are my grandchildren?"

"Fine, Julia."

"You know, I live for those grandchildren of mine."

As she hung up, Carol felt a sob rise from her gut, stick in her throat, explode out of her mouth, almost vomiting compassion for Julia.

Carol surfed quickly from channel to channel, hoping to catch the story on other local news stations. Glenda, your story has come and gone from the screen.

* * *

You would be proud of me.

I found his user's manual and I am teaching myself how to work the computer. I'm not as dumb as he thinks.

I was surprised to see that he has saved nothing in the general files part. So I am saving this on a file called "Test," so he will not open it. I trust in his lack of curiosity. But if he does, let him yell at me, too.

And if he asks, "What the hell is this?" I will give him back his own answer, "I need it in my work."

You'd be proud of me.

Carol liked to imagine that things were created out there in the mystery of cyberspace and that the whole human race can tap into them. Contact Bill maybe. Even her mother. If not now, later on, after access to the Information Superhighway becomes more fine-tuned.

"No, no, no!" Her father sounded exasperated. "You can retrieve from cyberspace only what has been entered into it."

After her father hung up, Carol keyed in "Bill Amber" anyway, a little defiantly, and got a stranger in Wyoming. What did you expect?

Tried Gordon. Got Gordon.

Tried James. Got James.

Both had Web pages.

Father? No.

Jack. No.

"Glenda has a Web site," she whispered aloud. "F has none."

Is a forensic computer analyst delving into your computer, searching for clues, Glenda?

Do *I* have a Web site, but don't know it?

Carol stopped.

Sorry. None of this applies to you, Glenda. I want to concentrate on you. I feel it in my bones that I am helping you. That seeing you so clearly, hearing you speak, watching your movements, and even listening to you think, talk to yourself inside your head, is really giving you another minute, another minute, another minute, and another hour.

* * *

Coming out of Big M supermarket, Melissa came to a sudden stop. "I want to *walk* back home."

"That would be nice, but what happens to the car?"

"Who's gonna steal that old junk heap?"

"If it weren't already mine, *I* would."

"I want to *walk* home."

"Oh, come on and get in the car."

"I want to *walk* home, please."

"Don't be silly, Melissa."

Melissa started walking.

Carol followed her in the car.

"Hey, you." No response. "Okay, be that way." No response. "So are you mad at me for a reason?"

Melissa shook her head no.

Melissa ran up the steep front steps as Carol parked the car uphill by the kitchen door.

Wandering around computer world in Jack's computer, I found what they call PERSONAL PHOTO FILE. It's full of obscene photographs, not only of men and women together. What would *you* do?

I guess everybody has a secret life. Even you. It's secret now, today, where you and F are.

I don't know whether his pictures are part of his routine life or one of those deviations the FBI keeps telling everybody to watch out for among our friends and relatives.

* * *

This is degrading. To Logan, to Tim, and to me. I hope Tim didn't see me looking so closely at him. For signs.

And don't go knocking at his door this time. Let them alone. They're children shut up together with their secrets. Even if it sometimes seems that there are no children anymore. That even at Melissa's age, they are all young adults, shut up in bodies that only resemble the children I knew, the child I was. Glenda, I wish I could check my impressions with Kendall. But I had no business going to her office with Melissa that time.

Should I offer them a cup of hot chocolate? Or is hot chocolate not cool? All out of Coke, or whatever they go for these days.

These days? How old are you getting to be, anyway, Carol?

Well, but if Logan gets too close to Melissa, shouldn't I be wary? Duty bound. But not so any of them notice.

Even so, it's only natural. But even so . . .

* * *

And now they are showing that sketch of the Daylight Serial Killer again—but now they call him only "a person of interest." They keep saying that if I see this man, do not approach him, he may be armed and dangerous. Call the task force 1-800-888-0000. Now they're saying F maybe has an accomplice. And they say maybe this car, no, maybe this truck, or this van—a different vehicle each time, seems like. Everything seems to turn out the way you would not imagine. The sketch is made up by profilers. A big maybe—a crude sketch of a Big Maybe. Be on the lookout for this Big Maybe, who may be armed and dangerous.

The TV says they took DNA from over a thousand men. No women. To rule them out, they said. They even came to the construction site, where Jack was helping to build what they call a residential hospice now, where you go when they finally tell you you are terminal. Like any man within a hundred miles, Jack could have been the one. But not now. Because F's with *you,* under your supervision, so to speak.

She turned away from the TV and sensed Tim following her into the kitchen, where she took a head of cabbage out of the refrigerator.

"I know who the Daylight Serial Rapist is. It's the boy who sits behind me and poots all the time."

Cutting the cabbage in two, Carol suppressed a laugh.

"I bet there's DNA even in a poot."

When she laughed, Tim looked at her as if she were a first-time visitor.

While Carol was still shredding cabbage, Tim came back in and sat at the kitchen table, as if waiting for her to laugh again.

Finally, he got up and ambled toward the door and turned and raised his hand for "so long."

I need to add LAUGH to my new TO DO list on the refrigerator. Maybe that's why he makes so much unnecessary noise. To smother the silence.

I hope he already likes girls. I hope he kisses one soon, and she chases him down and kisses him back, and then he comes home looking different, and like he wants to tell me he got kissed. I wish everything for him.

There I go, talking about me again. All day, I try to keep my focus on you, Glenda. It's a wonder I still have my wits about me.

* * *

Melissa laughing drew her into the master bedroom. She's always alert, not sad or withdrawn, but seldom falls into fits of laughter.

She is rolling around on Carol's bed and falls onto the floor, almost hyperventilating, watching a tangled threesome on fast-forward that Jack must have forgotten to eject from the computer in the walk-in closet.

Carol thought of a subtle ruse for getting Melissa out of the room. "Melissa, somebody is at the front door asking for you."

Melissa rolled over, backed down off the bed, and backed out of the room.

"Who is it?"

"Go see."

Melissa out of the room, Carol turned off the DVD porno, feeling guilty for playing a trick like that on a six-year-old.

"It's for you, Mother."

Disoriented by the coincidence, Carol rushed into the living room, where the front door stood wide open.

Well, Melissa was certainly not stupid. Nobody there but you, Glenda.

Melissa was twirling her long hair around her index finger, nonchalantly again, as if nothing were happening.

"Please stop doing that."

"Stop doing what?"

"Nothing. It's not your fault."

* * *

Having stumbled upon how to get a Yahoo e-mail account, Carol, with her basic proficiency at the keyboard, sought her father on the information highway, her first e-mail.

How many faces I see, see me? Each day?

How many faces I don't see, see me? Each day?

Alone, I am some sort of me.

You come in and replace me with your image of me, and I replace the you who replaces me.

The you that is you is surrounded by intimate yous—how father, husband, children see you—and public yous, hundreds who see you now and then or only once. You can consciously call up many, while the unconscious contains more than you can call up: all superimposed on one another, all active simultaneously.

An hour after Carol's e-mail, her father hit "Reply." "Don't stop."

But then when you remember that another term for it is "the net," or "the web," "a sense of disquietude hovers over you." My father demoted "The mass of men lead lives of quiet desperation" in favor of his own generalization. Once you make a connection with the Internet, are you caught forever in a net, a web? I mean, do things get into your mind that you wouldn't want in there, mysterious things, maybe mystical ones, that you cannot control, making more and more connections through phantom circuits?

* * *

When they got to the car door, Melissa pulled back, turned away.

"Forget something?" Melissa didn't speak. "I said, Did you forget something that you wanted to have with you in the car?" Melissa slowly shook her head. Carol opened the back door. "Then in you go." Melissa turned back toward the car, stopped, then backed away. "Go ahead and get in. . . . Why don't you get in car?" She shook her head. "What's come over you?"

"I don't know."

"It won't hurt you, will it?"

"I don't know."

"Will you please tell me what's wrong with your grandfather's old Oldsmobile?"

"It's not the car."

"It's not the car? Okay, then it's not the car. So what is it?"

"Nothing."

"Nothing, huh?" Carol squared off at Melissa and let silence seep into both of them until they stood stock-still, face to face. "Listen, kid, if it weren't such a blinding snow coming down, we could walk, but you know, it's only a short drive to Dockside and back. Okay?"

Melissa looked up at her. "Just to Dockside, then right back home?"

"Sure, that's all."

Melissa stepped up to the door, Carol opened it. Behind the wheel, she listened to Melissa fasten herself into the child restraint in the backseat.

In Dockside Pub, Carol repeated to Frank what she had just said to Glenda, because he was known to know computers.

"No, it's just the opposite, on that. From the first keystroke, *you* have total control, except for the pop-ups."

"Sounds like ordinary life. Total control, except for the pop-ups."

"Well, sure, you can look at it that way. . . . And so, on that. . . . No soup for me today. I'm cured of my cold now."

* * *

Driving up the hill toward the back door, she saw a man trudging up the steep steps to the front door.

From inside, she answered his knock.

"Come to see Jack."

"Jack's somewhere out there with the searchers."

"Oh, still looking for Glenda Hamilton?"

"No, now she—"

"Well, he was supposed to meet me at the Galloping Zebra Club."

"Tell me your name again."

"I'm Freddie."

"Jack never speaks about you, but I guess he has a lot of friends at the old watering hole that I don't know about. He doesn't talk much."

"Who, Jack? What's the old watering hole?"

"Oh. Well, that's where I thought he was going."

"He didn't say where he was going?"

"He doesn't always tell me exactly where he's going. He just goes, and suddenly, he's gone."

Freddie laughed. "That's a good one."

Shutting the door, she wondered where and what the Galloping Zebra Club was.

The phone rang.

"Is Jack home?"

"No, he is not. Is this Thyre?"

"You recognized my voice?"

"Of course, from you on the news. Want him to call you back?"

"Tell him we need him and his hovercraft on the hunt."

Jack came in looking exhausted.

"Did you meet up with that Freddie guy? He—"

"Yeah, finally. We got our wires crossed."

"What's the Galloping Zebra Club?"

"It's a guy thing."

"Oh. And since I am not a guy. . . ."

"No call for sarcasm."

* * *

The doctor is at death's door. That's TV news only because his wife is missing.

The doctors' nurses nursing the doctor, like the nurses nursed their fellow nurse —My mother's best friend dying of cancer in the very ward where she herself had nursed women dying of cancer for thirty years.

I want to help you all, your husband, all the women in all the hospitals and hospices and homebound sickbeds.

What a silly notion, Carol, my father said, that time I said something like that when my mother came home exhausted but exhilarated.

My mother just looked at me, seemed to understand.

114

You, too, perhaps, Glenda, have had such thoughts. Everyone seems so eager to say you are a loving person. But all the evidence points to you as a practical person, too, the person who gets the job done, does it well, and moves on to the next project.

But indiscriminate love is foolish, or so they say. Like the foolishness of God?

Children, only you, gathered around your father's bed, know what I am talking about, even though at this moment you can think only of him.

And what does Dr. Hamilton feel, there on the verge? Love? Fear? Resentment? Nothing? Nothing and everything?

Ironic, isn't it, Carol, my father would say to me—if only he would talk to me as he talks to hundreds of others—that as you are helping save the wife, the husband is dying, and you cannot help him.

When they are together on TV, gathered together in your living room, your daughters reel off their favorite memories of you. It makes them feel you are alive. And even after you have died a natural death decades from now, it will be that way.

I know how they feel. My own mother's presence is always here, in this house, I am steeped in it, and when I remember her getting into her noisy, starched nurse's uniform, she is much less dead. That time she came home all wilted-looking and shucked off her uniform as if it stung her and stepped into the shower, and I imagined her crying as the steam filled the room. "The smell of death . . . ," I once heard you saying to my father in your bedroom—at the half-open door. When you stepped out naked, you were as good as new. Was that that time or the other time? If I had two sisters, we could sort it out. Or maybe that would make it harder to pin down.

Sitting facing the mirror of the blank computer screen just before turning it on, she was only a step away from the bedroom, but she felt she was deep inside the closet, Jack's clothes in the left wing—distinct odor, some fumes from his work, toxic glues—her own clothes in the right wing—odors subtle but distinct, a slight scent of dry-cleaning chemicals—but in the middle, enfolding the "personal computer," his clothes and hers mingled, all of it distracting her from images of Glenda and F, until she plunged deep into her own words on the pale green screen.

Exploring along the information superhighway, I am on the highway with you, Glenda—well, back roads, some as raw as Indian paths that once actually were. You and F are exploring, too. Ways to escape—F from them, you from him, maybe even F from you, because you are such foreign territory to him.

Something about writing into a computer. I realize as I am *writing* that I am *thinking* less about you, talking to you less in my head, and "keying in" what's happening more often. What's that a sign of, I wonder? I've gone back to the beginning to "key in" everything I have been saying to you from the start, and I'm almost caught up to *now*. I am surprised that I remember so much of it, and I feel in each keystroke that I am more in control than when I was talking to you before, I feel that this way helps you more powerfully somehow, I don't know how. Hard focused, I guess. I'm almost to 116 pages. I "save" every page because I don't completely trust this machine not to "shut down" with a wink. But it's not just a machine, any machine, it seems there is more to it. The information superhighway takes you into some strange new territory. The wide-open spaces, like in the Old West or outer space.

Back to the news of the Daylight Killer, in a plastic wrapper in my front yard, on the slope where I always slip and slide in the snow.

But no mention of you. No mention of the shadow in our breasts. *Our* breasts. I am not the only one. How many in this whole wide world on the same day? Even my doctor—a young, lovely, supremely confident woman who told me she lives near me over in Orleans Four Corners—is a survivor. Why am I telling *you* all this? Because my surgery on Monday may expose unclear margins? And she is forced to cut again, and it invades the lymph system, the lymph nodes, and in a year or two I am gone? I am going now?

In spite of everything, in spite of everything, you and I are alive. And I still have my breasts, though one is mangled, and you have none. Your daughter Kendall—no, it was Lydia—let that slip right there on TV, that "it's so unfair he chose my mother, when she has had to suffer a double mastectomy." F does not know that, and you and I will keep him ignorant.

I have these feelings of guilt about you, Glenda. Like when I catch myself feeling that you are intruding. I have my own life to live, but you keep getting between me and it. The harder I try to keep you alive, the more I feel my own life, such as it is, slip away.

* * *

As they reach out with the needle, Carol, dreaming, whispers, Glenda, I'm sorry I won't be with you for a while.

After they give her a shot, Carol says, aloud to F, Please don't hurt her. Promise me you will leave her alone, F.

I promise.

Don't worry. We aren't going to hurt you.

—hurt, hurt, hurt. . . .

Leave her alone! You promised!

She wakes. F— F— F, did you hurt her?

You have abducted my abduction, Glenda says. You have abducted me and F as one. How dare you?

We're right here, honey. It's Jack.

She sees Tim at his side.

What happened while I was under?

Dr. Trenton speaks loudly, I think I got it all, Carol.

Where's Melissa?

Melissa, get out of that drawer.

Jack opened the drawer beside the hospital bed. Melissa was inside, asleep. She opened her eyes and blinked.

Carol sank again into sleep, hearing her own voice declare, You are your own abductor.

6

As I am still trembling from a nightmare about my coming surgery, you are trying not to be in this motel room, remembering, you are in New Mexico now, you are about Melissa's age again.

F sleeps beside you on the bed in a tourist court from out of the 1930s on the outskirts of a town you didn't even notice the name of, his arm across his face, as if to hide his shame.

Your left wrist cuffed to the bed.

He has not touched you since he shoved you into his black pickup. Maybe he can touch a woman only after he has cut her. And then the trembling thrill. And then the upsurge of revulsion. And then the waves of shame. And the violent resentment that she is what she is and she is almost not even that any longer, forcing him to search for another like her.

But for now, you look over at him, sleeping, looking no different from any other person the world over, early in the morning.

A nightmare is making his body jerk. He sits up of a sudden and shakes his head, and rubs his eyes, and heaves a sigh loud enough to wake you if you weren't already awake.

You have no plan. You are waiting for that one moment out of many imaginable moments.

He unlocks the cuffs for you to go to the bathroom. He trusts you, but only within an inch of your life. You keep the door cracked and check the mirror, hoping not to see him in it all of a sudden and you listen for that rusty cry the door makes and hope you don't hear it when you are sitting on the toilet seat or standing in the shower.

Barking drew Carol out of bed to the window. She knew now more keenly the different voices. Used to be, I'd hear barking, just barking, a fox barking like a dog, a wolf barking like a dog, a dog barking like a fox, a coyote barking like a dog, they were all dogs, barking. But now—that one, on the terrace of Boldt Castle, that's a coyote, declaring, I'm over here, come and catch me, if you can, ignorant of the fact that she is more domesticated than she knows.

* * *

With an the air of making a silent offering of a gift, Tim opened an old *National Geographic* in front of Carol on the prop for the recipe book: The Valley of Ten Thousand Smokes of Alaska. Without speaking, she picked it up, open as it was, and looked at it, as if looking for Glenda among the smoking vents in the ground, muttering, "She may be there, somewhere."

"Who?"

"What?"

"You said, 'She may be there, somewhere. . . .'"

"Oh . . . The girl of your dreams . . ." A lame cover-up. "I saw that coyote on the terrace over at Boldt Castle, Tim. It was quite a sight."

I'm glad I keyed this in, as they say. It's not about you. But I'm glad I keyed it in. Like family history on the fly. Sly.

* * *

"Please tell me the present condition of Dr. Denton Harrington. I am calling on behalf of his wife, Glenda."

"I regret that I am not allowed to divulge that information due to the patient confidentiality laws."

"Not even if I am her best friend?"

"Not even if you are blood kin. We have no way of knowing whether you are who you say you are."

* * *

Tim left out in plain view a poem about hearing hooves on the roof and going out into the yard and seeing in the moonlight, not the coyote but a gazelle on the roof ridge, walking, delicately balancing.

* * *

"Come, come, Melissa, get in the car, come, come!"

Carol did not find Melissa in her room, where more "discoveries" were continuing on the screen without her.

"No time for games, Melissa."

Walking briskly from room to room, Carol failed to find her.

"We need to get a move on, kid."

Not there.

Not there.

Where?

Maybe in here.

No.

"Not funny, Melissa. Do you hear me laughing?"

There she is, Glenda, in the last place anyone would think of looking. Under the flowered skirt of my mother's sewing-machine table.

Carol knelt and, holding the flowered skirt to the side, looked in at her. That's my daughter in there.

"Please tell me, Melissa, honey, what is it about the car that makes you afraid?"

"It's not the car."

"Then, for God's sake, what?"

"I don't know."

"You are a wise little child and I say you *do* know."

"I do not know."

"You can tell me."

"It's you."

"What?"

"You don't act the same."

"What on earth. . . ."

"You in the car, you're not the same."

"You're disorienting me, Melissa."

"Even in the house sometimes. Not the same."

"Same as what?"

"You don't act the same *you*."

"How don't act the same me? Tell me, tell me."

"You walk different—to the car, and when we get out and walk."

"I have no idea what—"

"Your voice sounds like somebody else sometimes."

On her knees, her head under the table with Melissa, Carol stayed silent a while.

"Well, we're just going a few blocks to the beauty parlor."

"We can walk."

"No, the ice is treacherous today, and they predict a blizzard coming, and we don't want to get caught in a blizzard, do we?"

Melissa uncurled herself out of hiding but shunned her mother's hand.

Carol and Melissa sat down in the beauty parlor that had just opened in the old jail, across from the Methodist church, in the shadow of the new water tower, blue, shaped like an inverted tear.

"Fix me up."

"How do you mean?"

"Just fix me up. I am a mess."

The stylist laughed. "Well, yes, but don't you have a style in mind?"

"Not really. When I thumb through those fashion magazines, I just think, That's other women. But why not me?"

"Basically, you have good hair. Let us be kind to it today."

"Let's. Melissa, are you content to watch?"

Melissa nodded wanly.

After he had done everything he could, the stylist whirled her around to get the gestalt, as her father would say. "Now, aren't we wonderful?"

"Yes. Wonderful."

"Doesn't she look wonderful?"

Melissa covered her eyes. "I can't look."

This one is for you, Glenda. This is where you would be this morning, if you could. In such a chair, but in Watertown, familiar fingers in your hair.

For me, personally, what difference does it make after I look at myself and we all say, Wonderful?

Isn't she walking oddly, Glenda—off balance?

"Mother, why can't we just walk home?"

"You know what they say, Why walk when you can ride?"

"Home's not far."

"Forgive me, Melissa. I didn't exactly tell you the truth. We did go to the beauty parlor, but now mommy has to go to Watertown again."

Melissa turned as if about to run. Carol took hold of her. "What's the matter with you lately? What is—the matter—with you?"

Melissa took a NO stance.

Carol opened the back door. "Get in this car."

Carol watched Melissa fall, slowly, into a deep silence, her body slumped like one of her dolls.

"Stop putting on an act."

Struggling to get her into the car felt like dealing with one of Tim's childhood tantrums in the supermarket. Melissa had never thrown one. But she wasn't squirming and twisting and sagging and kicking, the way Tim used to do. Melissa leaned back from the door, bone-stiff.

When Carol got an awkward but firm hold on her body, it was as if she was lifting a heavy rocking chair. Suddenly, Melissa broke into a kicking, screaming child, a storm that lured the hairdresser and his assistant out of the beauty shop to look. Carol finally turned her and shoved her into the backseat.

After she locked Melissa into the child restraint and locked all doors, back and front, and cringed at the furor, the fact struck her that her child had no one to turn to for help, not her brother, not her father, because her mother is all she has, and her mother is fearsome.

Ten miles outside of Alexandria Bay, she pulled over to the side of the highway and shut off the motor.

I am abducting my own daughter. Because I am caught up in my own circumstances, I am abducting my own daughter.

Trembling, she turned the key.

Buckled up by someone other than herself, Melissa fell totally silent all the rest of the way to Watertown.

"Walk ahead of me, please, Melissa, through that door. Thank you. Now just sit right over there with your toy. I probably won't be long."

There he sits. James.

Behind that desk of his, looking up at me.

Exactly the way he used to.

"What's the urgency after five years? I mean, this face-to-face thing, after stalking me for the past year or so."

"You didn't sic the cops on me."

"To be honest, Carol, I have enjoyed those glimpses of you."

"But this face-to-face thing is something else?"

"Well, yes, it is."

"I just had to see you do that thing with your fingers."

"Thing with my fingers?"

"Yes, the flexing and twittering, straight down at your side. I miss it. But don't you do it anymore?"

"A lot changes over the years."

"And too many things don't change in the least."

"So now you know. But speaking of change, are you still inclined to take one drink too many?"

"I've been clean for a year and two months. I don't drink. I drive."

"You find me in the midst of—"

"Were you really larger than life back then?"

"Come again?"

"Back then, I thought you were larger than life. Were you really?"

"Possibly, but probably not. . . . So . . . ?"

"I had a sudden need to know— What was it about me, James? In the beginning."

"Am I under oath?"

"This is a gray area."

"Lawyering thrives on gray areas. But this has to do with you, not the law."

"You said what I told you about me, about crossing northern Greece on my bicycle in the dead of winter, attracted you to me, and what I remember is that you asking all those questions, getting it all out of me, attracted me to you."

"I can say thus much: you telling me in the dead of winter in such great detail about your bicycle trip across Greece in the dead of winter— The contrast! This soft, wary girl who walked toward me slightly sideways, and who sat in my new-smelling Jaguar, telling me about tightening your spokes and adjusting your brakes and eating sardines out of a tin can and trudging up mountains for the view of the world below at dawn, fresh out of your sleeping bag, and you looking like a woman out of a play by Euripides— My God, I was *there,* with a fierce hard-on."

"I saw it. Wasn't taking off my clothes that did it, but my telling you about my trip, reliving it, your electric presence as the background?"

"Sounds about right."

"So, next, James, please tell me, please tell me what it was about me that made you choose her over me, I mean, aside from the fact we were both pregnant? Maybe by you."

"That was it, as I told you at the time. But—"

"But what? I came here for the big *but*—"

"You were overqualified, so to speak."

"What the hell does that mean?"

"You were the receptionist for a hotshot lawyer, when you could have been the hotshot lawyer herself."

"You never told me that."

"What would be the point of my telling you when you weren't telling yourself. You have to tell yourself and then go out and do it."

"I wish you had told me. You telling me would have motivated me."

"Unlikely. Besides—"

"Now we've come to the big *besides?*"

"It was almost too late, even then. And now—"

"And now, it *is* too late?"

"Frankly?"

"Yes."

"Frankly, yes."

"What would you say if I told you, I am determined to go back to Jefferson Community College and pursue a nursing degree?"

"You are breaking my heart, Carol. I am glad to see you again—although it probably was not such a good idea, and not one we should repeat—but you are breaking my heart."

Carol got up, saw John Updike's novel *Rabbit Is Rich* on his desk, and started out the door, but turned.

"Did you—do you know Glenda Hamilton?"

"Vaguely."

She did not see in his eyes what she had imagined she might see.

"Then, thanks for that, James." She took a deep breath. "And, let the record show that you were the love of my life."

Unwilling to hear James's response, Carol shut the door behind her and reached for Melissa's hand.

It's not that I failed to meet your great expectations, Father, but that you had no expectations, great or small.

"Melissa, we're starting home now, but before we get in that car, is there anything else on *your* mind?"

"Like somebody else is in there with us."

"Tell me."

"Sometimes two."

"You can tell me who."

"I don't know."

"Tell me."

"I don't know. One of them is a man maybe."

"Who?"

"I don't know."

"Does it scare you?"

"I'm scared."

"Tell me."

"Stop talking."

Let me take stock, Glenda. I have daily responsibilities and duties as a mother to a six-year-old girl child and an eleven-year-old boy child, plus I have daily and nightly responsibilities as a wife to a husband—in spite of all their daily complaints.

And when I look in the mirror, I can't help but notice that I still have one of the same enviable breasts that James used to call "the glory of Watertown."

Carol's body, all on its own, she felt, went so rigid, she pulled over to the shoulder of the highway, and forced her body to relax, until she began to cry, quietly at first, to avoid awakening and traumatizing Melissa.

Too late, too late.

Too late?

Back on the highway to Alexandria Bay, Carol imagined how Melissa, a child of six, must feel now, abducted by the circumstances—the people and

126

the places—of her short life. You have no choice. And even when you grow up and you do have a choice, and even if you have great ambition and march vigorously toward your goals in life, you will have had no choice but to have had me as your mother, to have had the brother and father you have now, and once other people and other places make up your life, you will have no choice because there it all is, even as you go into new places, new relationships. Abducted. Found in time—or too late.

You rear back and look at F. Maybe you'd better shave.

F feels his bristled cheeks.

He pulls into a Kwik Stop but just sits there, probably reluctant to take you in there with him, the gun concealed.

He moves the truck to the full-service pump and gets it filled up.

Say, fella, do me a big favor. Add a pack of disposable razors and bring 'em out with the receipt. Okay?

See how charming he can be, probably out of your influence. Even charming this young man.

Back on the road, you use your teeth to rip open the plastic razor bag for him. Is this your brand?

I ain't got no brand.

He is driving with one hand, dry shaving with the other, while you are using one on your legs, your pantyhose gone too many miles ago. I don't feel right, not shaving.

He uses whiskey for an aftershave and passes it to you. You dab it behind your ears and you decide to use whiskey from now on.

Who else knows about the bank?

Nobody knows about the bank, except me.

I trust you.

You know he doesn't.

Now you two are in the bank.

By now he is trusting you enough not to tell you how to act when you are together inside the bank, as if you two have done this before and know just what to do or have seen the same movies that have trained you how it goes. But you know he must have the buck knife and the revolver concealed somewhere handy.

He even stops right next to the guard. No, he's not a guard. He's a cop on his own time filling out a deposit slip. They don't use guards as such anymore.

You hope the manager will recognize your name from the news.

F sits beside you, waiting for the manager to return to her desk from on break.

The woman at the desk nearby offers you coffee, and you both say yes, with cream for you and black for him. But she gets it wrong, and he sips the coffee with cream, and you only pretend to sip because black makes you have to go and he always waits until he sees an unpaved road.

The manager appears, dressed like a movie star because she does not have the face of a movie star. But the more you look at her as she fills out the withdrawal form, with tiny flourishes of her head, her eyes, her mouth, her hands, her shoulders, even her hips that shift and settle in her chair, as if she is imagining what she could do with all that money if it were hers, the more attractive she seems. Does F watch her, does F see what I see?

No, the bank does not turn out to be the place where you can make your move. The manager is not startled to see your name, so maybe the news has not yet reached Staten Island. You have convinced yourself now that you can take your time for a while longer without serious risk. Unless, unless once he has the cash in the truck, his whole demeanor warns you that he has changed. Be vigilant, Glenda.

You withdraw all but two thousand, to deflect suspicion. The manager— not the one you opened the account with—may suspect something. All that money in cash, instead of a cashier's check or a wire transfer to another bank— a suggestion you turned down—may have started her thinking. Supposing. And when she looks at the two of you, what does she see? Man and wife? No, look at how you are dressed, the two of you. Lovers fleeing?

Or maybe two people who do not seem to know each other very well, two people who do not normally belong together. Your mannerisms and way of talking contrasted to his mannerisms and muteness. The once over. More than that?

As I watch you walk out of the bank, I have a question of my own. Why did you open that secret account on Staten Island of all places in the first place?

* * *

The whole world knows the power of pussy. Pussy power. So if, even after all this time, he finally does force you, fake it, make it something he never

128

fantasized could happen to him, so that he gets the impression you love it, and want it, again, again, and again, so that you disorient him, force him to into a whole 'nother realm where he is a stranger, doesn't know which way to turn, what to do next. A woman's form of rape? I don't know. What do *you* think?

* * *

What made him think he could do it to me? What made him think he could get away with it? And above all, What made it dangle? Fraternity rat Stanley Thornton was a virgin forcing himself to act macho—that could answer the first two questions.

As to the third question, perhaps he sensed all along it would turn out to be an exercise in futility because he saw something in her walk, her voice, her stance, her face that made him uncertain, especially when she gave him a look that intimated she was not the type to submit against her will, that her will would win out. And perhaps he was partly right, partly because she had to go to Greece to deal with even the lack of an outcome, because even his intent declared that he had seen her as being vulnerable when she had always assumed, needed to assume, that she was not, that she was in control of her life, day by day, and that that included moments like this.

Imagining how he must have felt then and over the years since made her feel compassion so gut-stirring, she surprised herself, saying aloud, "I forgive you, whoever you were."

She looked him up on the Internet. There was his picture online, at the Syracuse University Web site as an alumnus, right out of the yearbook.

A financial adviser. Terre Haute.

"Stanley Thornton speaking. How can I help you?"

May I help you. "You can help me by identifying this voice from the past."

"Ha. Sorry, I . . ."

"Are you really trying?"

"Ha. A name would help."

"Okay. Carol."

"Name, voice, nothing, sorry."

"Helvy. Syracuse University, 1992. Ha."

"Can I find you in the book?"

"What book?"

129

"Our yearbook."

"My education was rudely interrupted."

"Did I know you then?"

"In the biblical sense, no."

"Whatever that means. I don't mean to be rude, but—"

"You didn't say that then."

"When?"

"We were on a blind date."

"I should warn you that I have already won one paternity suit. For one thing, did you ever hear of a thing called DNA?"

"Listen, listen to me. Listen. I just called up to tell you that it swept over me this morning somehow that an amateur, humiliated rapist must live with that failure all his life."

"I'm hanging up."

"I hate to play with words with you at this point in time, Stanley, but that was sort of the problem. It was just hanging there."

"I don't get it."

"You won the struggle and I lay on the floor of your frat room looking up at you, and you had one foot on my left wrist, and even though it just dangled above my head, I was terrified."

"The statute of—"

"No, no, no, no, I worked for a lawyer who was larger than life, and—But let me finish. I was about to tell you why I wanted to call you, and that is, I want you to know that I forgive you."

"I accept . . . whatever. . . . And now, if you will—I have a client in the waiting room and I really must be excused."

"Did you talk that way back then?"

"Really, I don't—"

"Okay, just one more thing and you may go. A question. A three-part question, as in our introduction to basic sciences class."

"I'm listening, but I must tell you, you have the wrong—'

"One. What made you think you could do it? Two. What made you think you could get away with it? And three. What made it dangle?"

Did the limp "member" express his fear of her power to reject him? Or did that limp "member" thing express *his* rejection of *her?*

Stanley Thornton hung up.

I am right back where I started.

* * *

Her father stopped by on his way to spend an evening with his friend Wylie at Hart House on Wellesley Island. Or maybe a woman. Maybe even somebody's lovely wife.

"Father, I got something for you."

He stood akimbo in the door frame, looking at her askance.

"Shoot."

"You are not looking at my face—over here, look at my face, Father. Okay. Now, notice that I am looking at your face."

Her father did an old vaudeville comedy reaction routine, hand to his cheek, looking slow right, slow left, then up, as if for help.

"Cut it out, please, and listen. Okay. You see my face, among thousands you have seen and will see in your lifetime. But can you see your own face? Can I see my own face? As we look at each the other's face?"

His face showed he was getting it. But he shrugged, lifted his eyebrows, mugged.

As he turned away, did he have any inkling that in shrugging off her gift of an insight, he had hurt her feelings?

Having given him time to visit Hart House, then get back home, Carol punched in his number.

"When I offered you what I assumed was a rather original psychological insight with possible far-reaching implications, you shrugged—you literally shrugged—it off. And so I am calling, because I was just wondering *why.*"

He interrupted her voice message.

"Only my way of expressing my surprise that you had forgotten."

"Forgotten what, may I ask?"

"Oh, don't be Miss Prim. Forgotten the fact that I had told you about that phenomenon years ago, when you were about to go off to college."

"Is that another one of your—?"

"You may not remember, but *I* do, and I even remember that you got into it."

"Oh. Well. Sorry. Well, at least I didn't totally forget, did I?"

* * *

131

Needing to be with Glenda, responding to a compulsion to drive over the International Bridge into Canada, Carol got in the car alone, feeling alone, leaving Melissa behind like that, with Tim to watch over her. She felt she must free Melissa of herself for a while. The window open to the stinging cold cleared her head. Is that a dog strolling on the Bridge? Too far to tell. Wild one, or tame one? Wolf maybe? That coyote? Too big for a fox, so not our cat either.

You had a life most women would envy. Even with your sick husband, it has been better than most. And not only do you achieve good things in the eyes of the public, you are (they are saying *were* now, but I will never say *were*) a very likable person. It's all just as I imagined while I was watching you at the lighthouse. In those frozen three minutes, I imagined it all, like seeing your own life as you are drowning. Not the details, which in your case were—are—full of God, but an impression that thrilled my soul. You are my hero—my heroine—doing what you are doing now. You are waiting to get him in a crowd—the bank was under populated—or an intersection clogged with traffic, watching for him to drop his guard. Your scream is as loud as any woman on earth, even though you probably never had to use it, except maybe outdoors in a football stadium, in a special box, glassed in among all your artistic, rich, and political friends.

* * *

Her father left a voice message: "Daughter, your father used your insight on 240 Intro to Psych students, my night class a while ago. It was a big hit."

As an afterthought, another message a little later. "And yes, the psychological question raised is, What effect does that human condition have on human behavior? I seek an answer."

Even as she felt elated, his condescending tone placed her at a low level. To hell with you, professor.

What was *your* father like, Glenda?

* * *

"Grandpa left a strange voice message." Tim looked at the phone as if it might speak.

"I'm not surprised."

Pretending lack of interest, Tim left the room.

"I must confess to you. The idea did not originate with me. One of my own students told me years ago, and she said she got it from Luigi Pirandello's novel *One, No One, and One Hundred Thousand.* It's the whole novel, about that. Bye."

Tim came back into the room. "Who's Pirandello supposed to be?"

"I think he was Italian. Wrote plays too, I think."

"I could look him up on the Web."

"Your mother could tell—Yes, do that."

Her father would be home now, sitting at his desk, grading that lifelong procession of papers. She remembered finally putting his Christmas present to her in the glove compartment, the cell phone. She sneaked outside to key him in, sitting in the car.

"I saw the missing lady."

"In what sense?"

"And I talk to her every minute, even as I am talking to you now."

"Give me time to calibrate that, Carol, and let's talk later, maybe tomorrow."

* * *

I had to get off the computer just now—I'm up now to the part where you take him into your bank on Staten Island—because it's on TV now that they think they have a suspect. Not white, as in that man-from-Mars sketch. Now he's black, and his sketch looks like the man in the moon. Will he even recognize himself? If he happens to see it, he would probably heave a sigh of relief, thinking it's somebody else.

"A woman who would not let us show her face on television told Eyewitness News she was attacked in her kitchen but drove the intruder away with a pair of scissors."

He was not driving that rust-bucket black pickup shrouded in snow but a gold-colored car, they are saying, but which looks white to me on the TV.

"Officials speculate that the assailant may have access to several vehicles from different sources, perhaps in more than one town in this region."

They have stopped talking about *you* on Jack's big TV. Maybe you don't count anymore because of the aftermath of the snow blizzard and the war in Iraq. I miss seeing Paulette talking about you. Everyone has forgotten you. I promise you, Glenda, I promise you, I will never forget you.

I wonder. Is someone somewhere in this world talking to me the way I am talking to you? My father, the mind reader, who lives a life of the mind? Is he of two minds, does he talk to me, so that when he sees me in the flesh, he has exhausted all subjects of conversation?

Even Jack? What life am I living with Jack that only *he* knows?

Hearing the noise of the fun-loving air boaters rallying, she knew what had awakened her. That and maybe Melissa, who stood in the doorway, looking at her.

I dreamed last night I domesticated the coyote, Glenda. But it saddened.

And then I looked behind the television in the family room and it was dying.

Like Melissa, who had no choice of mothers, who had no choice but to get into her car, night after night, time after time, I have been abducted, from childhood until now, by circumstances, this place, Alexandria Bay, the Thousand Islands, and Watertown, and these people, my father, my mother, the men in my life before the children and the husband in my life, all those fluid-fixed relationships.

7

Where *are* you?

Where *are* you?

Where *are* you?

Another young career woman is missing! Marita Wahl may become a mere number—nine.

What happened to *you?*

I am trying not to be of a doubtful mind, Glenda.

They think it may be the Daylight Serial Killer, but if it is, who took *you?* Maybe it's a different killer. They say it could be a copycat. They say it could be somebody she knew. Her name is Marita, thirty-seven years old. She is the owner of a classy dress shop in Salmon Run mall. Marita Wahl. They said she was very friendly and very smart. Just like you, only younger. Marita. Marita Wahl. Now *all* the mothers are calling for a march on the courthouse, this time the federal one, demanding action.

But who took *you?*

Where *are* you?

They won't know if his DNA matches hers until they find Marita's body.

I don't know what to think. I can't imagine.

I'm sorry. I'm sorry! You expect too much from me.

As Carol watched clouds moving across the sky, they picked up speed. "Stop!"

* * *

"Early this morning, searchers on snowmobiles found the Wahl woman's body on Heart Island. They looked inside Germanic Alster Tower, where the Boldt family lived while Boldt Castle was being built. The Wahl woman was found in the beautiful Venetian room, posed, like all the others, in an elegant chair. The killer left no trace."

Jack raised his voice at the TV. "Those imbeciles will never catch him. They're smart. Very smart. All hundred or more of them, minus me. I got disgusted and parked my iceboat. That Thyre thinks she's— All they are ever able to do is go to the place where ice fishermen or kids skating find tracks that lead to a house where he breaks in and sets up the bodies. How much intelligence does that take?"

He isn't asking *me*. He's asking the TV.

Everybody's mad. All seven mothers and the new one are on TV again, mad as holy hell. They're calling for another rally, on the federal courthouse steps again.

This discovery opens the case against all husbands all over again. I am forced, like most wives, to review his entire history for signs. He's not the one with you, so F could be any woman's husband, if he indeed has a wife, which he probably does. The profiler came on TV and listed all the signs to look for again. Makes me feel a certain oneness with wives. If you were not missing and your husband were not confined to his deathbed, you would wonder, too, wouldn't you? My husband catches me looking at him and gets this quizzical look on his face. Does he wonder whether I am noticing how handsome he is? Well, he's not. But he could think so. Women say the suspect is charming with women. That lets you off the hook, Jack. But then there's my own father, who is charming to everybody but his next of kin. You never know, do you? Sure, my husband could have been the one. Any one of them could have been the one. It's the damned not knowing.

More apprehensively than usual, Carol opened the refrigerator. She put things in and took things out, but Jack only took things out. Why did that make it more his than hers?

* * *

"—Hamilton was considered one of the region's leading surgeons. He died of lung cancer last night at the age of sixty. His wife of fifteen years, civic leader Glenda Hamilton, is still missing."

You'll miss your husband, but maybe not watching him wasting away. You felt guilty realizing that, but now you have a reason. Even so, you are glad you do not have to see him. That makes you feel guilty all over again. If he were my husband, how would I feel? I can't imagine.

But before, you and I could have died of the "secret, silent killer." That makes us see everything differently, doesn't it? Bad things are not as bad as they could be, and good things are like extras. But this coming Monday in the OR will be another story for me. Will my mother be there?

I miss you, Glenda. I can't imagine where you are now. I refuse to think F could have killed you that very night. "The first two hours are crucial."

I rejected the two-hour rule and the twenty-four-hour rule and the two-day rule, and now that we are into the eighth day, I violently reject, so to speak, the one-week rule.

You have been the best thing in my life.

That's terrible to say, since I have a husband and two children and I see my father sometimes.

Father sailed by here today on his way, I suspect, to see a lady friend somewhere on Wellesley Island—he mentioned the International Bridge—and be witty and charming. Promised we would talk about me and you maybe tomorrow or next week, Monday after his night class when he might come to visit me in Samaritan Hospital.

"I must confess that I have never really understood you. But now after all these years, I think I have nailed you down: you have the compassionate imagination, you are, in fact, an empath, a rare achievement."

"What's an empath?"

"Look it up."

* * *

137

And then there's *me*. I have *me*. And knowing you has made me feel more alive than I have felt since I was a kid, when I was talking to you, seeing you and F all day long and into nighttime reveries that put me to sleep—about the whole gamut of future possibilities. Now I feel alive to everyone and everything about me. You gave me a purpose. Even a mission. To help you save yourself. And who can tell me that I have not? We have been of one mind, striving together.

* * *

"It's A Match!" The Sunday morning paper's front-page headline. DNA found on Marita is the same as found on Theresa, Lorna, Ashley, but not yet matched to Courtney, Kaleesha, and Danielle.

And there's his actual face, a formal photograph, not the not-quite-human sketch. A tall, slender, handsome black man.

The morning news showed a woman who knew him. "He was always very charming and friendly. He gave me a rose one time, right out of the blue." *Was,* as if he is already on his back, strapped to the table, the needle in his vein, the warden tapping his foot and looking at his watch.

They say this "gentleman" has often been arrested, but only for petty crimes, several years ago, and so they didn't profile him as a possible rapist-killer. If they can match his DNA with that found on *all* the other women, he'll be more than just "a person of interest" that they want to question "in connection" with the rape he got caught attempting yesterday. He's even married and has five kids, owns a house in the Watertown suburbs, works for the railroad, and is a churchgoer.

F is on the loose.

* * *

Why is F headed toward the Pine Barrens of New Jersey?

Everything is confused. And now so am *I*.

Melissa is distracting me with something she found in the back yard. Is that a kitty cat in her arms?

"Can we keep her?"

"How do you know it's a her?"

"I just know."

I have to go. Melissa needs me. I must tell her about strange cats, even kittens. Carriers of disease, mange, rabies.

She has a scratch on her arm.

I can't imagine what happened to you after F drove into the Pine Barrens. Am I deserting you when you need me most? Maybe F is on an even keel, just before some storm suddenly rises up in him, like they report on the Great Lakes. I need to stay close by.

For now, you are safe, Glenda. Please don't worry. I promised never to leave you.

"Come out in the yard, Melissa. Bring the kitty cat." F's on an even keel right now. Don't worry. I won't let him—I won't let him—You— "Drop the kitty cat before she scratches you again!"

"It doesn't hurt."

"Yes, it does. Yes, it does! It hurts. It hurts!"

"What's the matter, Mother? Where're you going?"

Carol stayed down in the basement awhile, among the shelves of her mother's preserves, going through the motions of choosing, but then remembering the last moment of her mother's life down here.

Woods on the left and woods on the right, and not a single car behind or ahead for five or ten minutes at a time. One country road after another, left and right. ROAD ENDS. Back up and try another road. The smell of cold pine trees as the two-lane highway swings this way and that way. But the Pine Barrens are so close to Manhattan they say that at night you can see the lights of the Empire State Building.

Now you are nervous and hope he can't tell.

F seems on an even keel. But seems is not always so. So . . .

Breakfast dishes cleared away, Carol turned around twice in the middle of the kitchen, stopped, seeing Melissa in the doorway, the kitten draped over her shoulder.

"No more of those trips in the car, honey. I promise. Feel better now?"

"Starting to."

"Well, a start is a start."

"You go first."

"Take my hand." Saying that most Sunday mornings, Carol heard her mother say to her, "Take my hand."

Melissa took her hand.

"Take my hand, Tim."

"Oh, Mom." Almost two years stretched between her gentle command and Tim's first refusal to take her hand, but she said it anyway, and felt Tim was reluctantly glad she did.

As they set out from the house and passed the fortress-like Catholic church, she felt drawn, as always, toward the rock, the rock itself, on and into which her church was built.

The ice-fishing derby had ended, but men and women sat out there on wooden crates on the ice, lines dangling above sawed-out holes, just left and right of Boldt Castle.

Tim walked ahead with his father, who was a creature of habit. Sunday church without fail, except when he did.

Carol heard someone say Reverend Sensibar may retire young. She ministers to two churches in two different villages and drives from one to the other and then home to kids. What gives her the right to retire? I ask you, Did Jesus retire? Well, yes, I guess, in a way, he did, didn't he? Early.

"It is a custom started by ancient Christians to greet one another, saying, 'Peace be with you.'" Reverend Fredrika Sensibar raised her arms. "Let us stand now and greet our neighbors. God knows, you may make a new friend this morning. We are small in number, but big in heart."

As they passed the peace, members and visitors, among whom Carol included Glenda and F, and shared "concerns and celebrations," mindful that this was the second Sunday in Lent, Carol felt the Holy Spirit in this place more intensely than usual. We are in the mind of the Spirit.

"Paul to the Colossians, three, three: 'For ye are dead, and your life is hid with Christ in God.'"

Hearing the voice, Carol looked up to see the face. My neighbor, Mrs. What's-her-name. No. No. No. Mrs. . . . Mrs. Garrison. Wife of George, the butane delivery man.

As she joined, a little loudly, in saying the Lord's Prayer, she sensed Jack look over at her, Tim sink his head into his shoulders, but Melissa squeezed her hand on "trespass" and raised her own volume a decibel or two.

When Reverend Sensibar called the children to gather around her before the altar, Melissa, stepping on Tim's toes, rushed to get there first.

"Who wants to take a bite of this rotten apple?" Reverend Sensibar was holding a rotten apple out, waving it back and forth. "All right, then, who is willing to take a bite of this luscious apple?" She brought forth from behind her back a luscious apple, held it high.

Having gone through some miserable moments up there herself as a child with a few other ministers, Carol sometimes regarded Reverend Sensibar's children's messages as inspiring as her sermons.

An embarrassment to Tim and sometimes to Jack, Melissa was usually a delight, answering questions that often enabled her to tack on questions of her own. Anticipation made Carol sit erect in shivering expectation.

Reverend Sensibar posed questions about food that is good for you and food that is bad for you, leading up to a spiritual question that Melissa had squirmingly anticipated. The other six children lowered their upturned faces and turned to Melissa, who finally said it. "The fruits of the flesh are rotten, but my daddy says the fruits of the spirit are damn good for you."

Laughing, the congregation turned and looked at Jack, who raised his right hand as if in witness and shyly added, "Amen."

Standing, singing "I Need Thee Every Hour," Carol felt Glenda's spirit in this place.

"Seek Ye First" sung, Reverend Sensibar's sermon "expatiated," as her father would have said, upon the verse "I Am the Bread of Life," the everyday connection being the abundance of expressions that employ eating—"chew you out, bite your head off, fed up, drink it all in." Reverend Sensibar ended her sermon with a litany of other New Testament applications. "Now that Christ is pure spirit, his body gone from this earth, isn't it almost beyond imagining that we are the body of Christ, not figuratively but literally, for his body is dead, but he lives only in our living bodies."

Which means that I am not terminally biological.

"It is cold, even for February, and the unrelenting snow and ice are treacherous, and so we are few here this morning, but though some may sleep, we who are awake must speak the Word. Therefore, go forth now as a light, and gently but firmly wake up those who sleep in the dark. Let us all strive together to be of one mind, having compassion for each other. Remembering what Paul wrote to the Hebrews (12:1). 'We are compassed about with a great cloud of unseen witnesses. . . .'"

What does she know?

"And I will raise him up at the last day" rang in her head all the way home.

* * *

You are driving, lost in the Pine Barrens, getting very sleepy.

F is asleep. But is he? Could be a test. Don't worry. You will pass it. Like every test you ever took, from grade school on up through the university. You can't cram for a test like this one. It all depends on who you already are. And you, Glenda, have prepared for this one all your life, and your life depends upon it. So far, so good. Test him.

You come to a slow stop beside the highway.

F is still asleep.

Closing your eyes, you lean your head back and rest.

After a few minutes, you hear him stir.

Are you awake?

I've been awake ever since you took the wheel.

You were testing him, and he sounds as if he is content that you have passed his own test.

You rest the full five minutes they say you need. Then you drive on.

The Pine Barrens, the Discovery Channel says, is a maze.

* * *

They ask, What was she doing at the lighthouse?

They wonder, Did she just let herself slip down into Lake Ontario?

Was her childhood sweetheart, the love of her life waiting for her there, they wonder.

Some imagine you brutally dead and secretly buried.

You are every place people want you to be.

I choose to settle for what a young woman in our drugstore on Highway 12 imagines, whispering her opinion to an older man she seems to know.

"Well, personally, *I* think she's alive, like, in Paris or London or, like, Rome— probably Rome. She looks, like, Greek. Alive and well and, like, rich. Faked her abduction and, like, split. I met her once. I wouldn't put it past her. I *hope* she's, like, in Rome. The Italians would love her to pieces. Just look at her."

And the older man's gaze turns inward, as if he is seeing you there, throwing the coin for luck over your left shoulder into that famous fountain.

But they say that whenever you were having a tough time you'd go, "I'd rather be in Paris."

They say you said that often, and it always got a big laugh, because they knew you liked to say it and they liked to hear you say it. They say you'd say, "I'm having a wonderful time running for the city council, folks, but I'd rather be in Paris!"

Are you?

Are you?

I hope so.

I wish I could be in Paris with you and stand beside the flame of the unknown soldier under the Arch of Triumph.

But I have an appointment tomorrow morning in Watertown that I cannot miss.